VICTIMS

A Tale From Fermanagh

by

EUGENE McCABE

THE MERCIER PRESS

DUBLIN and CORK

The Mercier Press Limited
4 Bridge Street, Cork
25 Lower Abbey Street, Dublin 1.

First published by VICTOR GOLLANZ LTD.
This edition by THE MERCIER PRESS LTD, 1979

Reprinted 1979

ISBN 0 85342 592 2

For Margôt

LEONARD WAS LEANING on the rail of the jumping enclosure watching the entrance. Music had been coming from the speakers since he arrived—"Land of Hope and Glory"—now competing with the staccato of cantering, jumping horses, the bawling of show cattle, megaphoned instructions from stewards, the squealing of pigs, sudden bursts of applause, the continuous hubbub of talk within and without the licensed marquee.

On a pole above the marquee a Union Jack flapped in the south wind. From it triangular bunting in red, white and blue stretched round the enclosure taking in the judges' platform and a small committee tent. Across the entrance from the road an embroidered cloth read:

WELCOME TO INVER SHOW

GOD SAVE OUR QUEEN

Dark-suited countrymen in hats, caps and boots, their wives in capacious summer wear and strong shoes examined pens of sheep, pigs and fowl, inspected and criticized glossy, prize-winning show cattle, walked through covered stalls of garden and domestic produce, argued cheerfully with salesmen about the merits and defects of gleaming new tractor models and agricultural machinery, or sat about in family groups eating sandwiches, whip-ices or drinking beer in the August sun.

Here and there, jodhpurs, tweed and blatant voice, or casual urban wear allied with a Yorkshire accent marked the presence of gentry, their guests, and British soldiers on unobtrusive day-leave from barracks at Lisnaskea or Roslea.

Nothing much had happened. A horse had broken its leg. Leonard had heard the vet. say quietly to the owner:

"It'll have to be destroyed."

As the last horse cleared the jumps he kept watching the entrance with his good eye. Beyond the show-ground the sloping meadows of after-grass gave way to the grey-brown brooding of Fermanagh uplands. In the long view detail seemed blurred. In the enclosure a fresh crop of dandelions crocheted in the green sward pulsed with a violence that forced him to look away. He covered his eye with a scarred hand, took out a scrap of paper, read the coded message without expression, put a match to it and dropped the blackened ash.

When he looked up she was in the entrance, waiting, a smallish madonna, composed, with cool all-seeing eyes, her face set in a medieval mould. He waited till she moved, then left the railing and went towards her. Unsmiling, Lynam watched him approach. He had grown a beard which hid the aggressive jut of his lower lip. They did not shake hands as she said:

"It's you."

"Yes."

"That much I was told."

A city girl dressed for summer streets, leather shoulder-bag and sandals. From a battery-powered megaphone a steward announced twice: "All winning competitors in the beef section to the judges' stand."

Leonard guided her through the crowd past farmers urging a nervous Friesian bull up the ramp of a trailer, down a grass alley-way of farm produce and display stands towards an open space at the rail of the jumping enclosure directly opposite the judges' platform. He reached in the pocket of his denim jacket for cigarettes. When they were both lit his silence forced her to speak.

"For a friend you are not saying much."

"Nor you."

"I know nothing except ..."

She paused for the megaphoned voice to announce: "Armstrong Memorial Award for the best beef bull: Samuel Foster of Mullinahone."

When the ragged applause faded she said: "A car called at four, an Army Council note, I was to go where I was taken, didn't say where ... under your command ... Burke's hand ... and the driver said nothing between here and Dublin. That's all I know."

After another announcement she said: "I was very frightened ... still am."

"Of what?"

"A final journey."

"Nothing like that."

"You've been briefed, warned, something."

"I don't believe all I hear."

"You take orders."

"Don't you?"

She paused before asking: "What orders?"

Another announcement greeted with back-slapping and laughter, a popular winner.

"Big house," Leonard said. "We hold some gentlefolk till they bring us Quinn, McIntyre, and Fanin from Long Kesh."

"What big house?"

"Inver Hall, two miles from here ... that's him," Leonard said, with a jerk of his head towards the judges' platform. "I don't want to point, the tall one, jodhpurs and cloth cap."

"Who's he?"

"No one ... the young one's his son-in-law. Secretary, Foreign Office."

As Lynam shrugged Leonard added: "Also he's an English lord."

Lynam stared across the enclosure: "When?"

"Tonight."

There were three more announcements before she spoke: "They won't release them."

"They'll think about it."

"And if not?"

"We keep our word."

"How?"

"Does it matter?"

"Will that involve me?"

"You'll be there."

The spikey growth of bladed grass at her feet seemed terrifying in the golden light. She could feel sweat going down her back.

"And if they bring them?"

"We leave."

"With the gentry?"

"Till we're clear."

"Where to?"

"That's fixed."

"And if they refuse?"

"I've said it."

For a moment she hesitated before saying: "Kill them?"

"Execute."

"Then what?"

"We fight."

"It's suicidal."

"Simple and works elsewhere."

She paused to ensure that her voice would not betray what she felt.

"I didn't volunteer for active service, why me?"

Leonard shrugged.

"Policy?"

"He, they ... someone wants rid of me ... you ... have you thought of that?"

"Like?"

"Burke."

Leonard thought about this then shook his head.

Lynam asked: "And if I refuse now?"

Leonard dropped his cigarette on the grass and covered it with his foot, and asked with more concern than threat: "Can you?"

When Lynam did not reply Leonard asked: "Drink?"

"No."

"Sandwich?"

She shook her head.

"Tea?"

"No ... thanks."

"Ice?"

To stop the persistent questions, sort out the awfulness of what he had just told her and steady the unnatural racing of her heart she nodded assent.

She followed him as he made his way towards the whipped ice machine. A woman in charge was adjusting something at the back.

"Two please," Leonard said.

"In a minute," the woman said.

Leonard nodded and moved away a few yards. As they waited Lynam looked at him properly for the first time.

"What happened to your eye?"

"Accident."

"On a job?"

"Yes."

"Can you see with it?"

"No."

"I'm sorry."

He nodded and said: "And me ... for your trouble."

Her face gave nothing away. "Not much you don't hear."

When he made a gesture she said: "Abortion is the word."

Her mind, he thought again, a clenched fist against pity, maidenhood, motherhood or anything denoting feminine softness. She had climbed fast and high, in a movement dominated by power-hungry men, unafraid of violence and now unsure of her motives. Some felt she secretly despised them and the cause. Drunk once in a Rathmines flat Burke had told him:

"She knows too many dodgy Press boys and politicians ... calculating as a cat ... makes love with her eyes open ... Christ knows what she thinks or believes ... not in me ... not in God ... I've even wondered if she's Special Branch, but I think not."

At the time Leonard was amused at Burke aligning himself with God, but felt the assessment of Lynam was fairly accurate. He was tempted now to say something unkind. He said:

"It's a bleak word."

She looked at him steadily for a moment. Like other Northerners she'd met, close; spare with words.

"Almost," Burke had said, "as clever as me."

The reply in her mind did not reach her mouth. She looked over at the woman filling cones and said:

"Your whips are ready."

A blond man, almost albino, with a tall limber Negro, both in vivid shirts and jeans, approached the ice-cream stand unaware of Leonard. The Negro spoke:

"Can you give us two love?"

The woman said, nodding towards Lynam and Leonard, "These were here first."

The Negro turned: "Sorry mate."

"That's OK," Leonard said.

As they walked away Lynam asked the question with her eyes. Leonard nodded.

"What does he think of it over here?"

"Who?"

"The Negro."

"He doesn't think, he reads the gutter press."

A tinker woman carrying an infant wrapped in a rug blocked their path. She had reddish hair, bad teeth, glazed eyes, and looked years beyond child-bearing.

"God bless you Sir, Miss, can you spare a copper for a poor baba?"

The child, Lynam thought, looked pallid and sick. As Leonard groped for a coin she asked: "What age is your baby?"

"Near three months Miss."

The Colonel approached from the right, and said to her: "You're welcome my dear but I've already told you twice ... you must not beg from people."

"Yes, your Honour."

As she moved away the Colonel said to Leonard: "Not charity to give when she spends it all in there."

He nodded towards the licensed marquee. The Colonel looked directly into Leonard's face then into

Lynam's eyes. As he moved off he said: "Lovely day."

"It is," Leonard said.

As they watched him walk away Lynam asked: "Do you want to kill him?"

"You know the answer, why ask?"

They walked in silence to the enclosure where Lynam asked: "Deadline?"

"Tomorrow midday."

"If they refuse ... what?"

She stopped, unable to frame the question. Leonard answered: "One on the hour ... then one every six hours."

Lynam looked at the whipped ice. A squirt of liquid raspberry on top had run down the cone onto her fingers. She had not tasted it and looked at it now with revulsion.

"How many?"

"Six or eight most nights to dinner."

"I don't want this."

Leonard took her whipped ice.... Everywhere farmers were loading livestock onto trailers and lorries. The Show was over but the presentation of rosettes continued at the judges' platform, punctuated by announcements and scattered clapping. From the speaker the melody of "The Eton Boating Song" was drowned by the sudden slash of horse-piss on grass as a brown gelding straddled comfortably about ten yards from where they stood. Lynam asked:

"Must we endure this?"

"We can go any time."

Making their way towards the entrance they passed stalls of garden and domestic produce flanking the marquee. A tall woman with a well structured face and beautiful limbs surrounded by farmers' wives was saying with careful articulation:

"My mother used to add lemon verbena to crab-apple jelly; gives it a wonderfully subtle flavour."

Leonard said quietly, "His wife."

"Whose?"

"Colonel's."

"She'll be there tonight."

Leonard nodded and Lynam said: "She reminds me of someone."

They walked out of the show-ground, got into a black beetle Volkswagen and drove south towards the border.

THE COLONEL HAD shaken many hands, dispensed rosettes, certificates, trophies, Perpetual Cups and Medals of Merit. As he moved towards Alex Boyd-Crawford, George Hawthorne, blacksmith and small farmer approached:

"George?"

"A word Sir."

George was serious. He had been questioned, the Colonel knew, by the R.U.C. in connection with a double murder three miles from Inver. His nephew Eric O'Neill, a boy of twenty-three and part time soldier in the U.D.R., had been accidentally shot at an Army check-point; suicide it was rumoured.

Glazed by grief and whiskey the eyes that stared from that anvil-grey face looked someway blind. The Colonel was prepared to listen briefly:

"Something over here I want you to see," George was saying and began to walk.

"Yes?"

He was pointing a calloused finger at the dry closet left of the entrance with "Gentlemen" printed over the door.

The Colonel stopped:

"Can't you tell me George ... some obscenity?"

"I'll say it straight Sir ... one of our 'patrons' shit

on the floor and writ above it, 'That's what we think of the Brits and their Army ... up the I.R.A.'"

The Colonel's expression did not change.

"Words."

"Animals ... turn your stomach."

"Words, George."

The Colonel looked away to a helicopter hovering over the field and forest uplands of Roslea:

"People are being murdered every day."

"*You* tell me that Sir ... then I'll tell you ..."

Harriet's nervous laugh came across the enclosure. She had been to the licensed tent before midday. Dinner would be awkward again this evening. He missed what George was saying, then heard:

"O'Donnell from the Show committee ... he's one of them ... and they're all like that ..." he clenched his fist, "agin us."

The Colonel looked into George's eyes. The fist gesture was both ridiculous and menacing. Aiden O'Donnell, a solitary Catholic on the Inver Show committee, was an English-schooled, week-end farmer, and a full-time barrister, his Jesuit brother on the teaching staff of Stonyhurst, another brother director with a Belfast merchant bank. O'Donnell had once said, "I must argue for justice in a system I think unjust. Most of the time I feel hypocritical." A disloyal statement? From a Northern Irish Catholic warmed by liberal wine, a predictable one. The Colonel understood both George's demand and O'Donnell's dilemma.

"George, you must understand ..."

"O'Donnell goes or I quit ... and you'll find another to shoe your horses."

The Colonel shook his head. As he tried to find a moderate reply, George turned and walked away. The Colonel watched him go. In comparison with such complexities war was a simple discipline, no weak links in the chain of command, deserters shot, the enemy destroyed, no confusing allegiances, no references to root causes, no twingings of conscience. In an unsubtle way George was right. O'Donnell had refused the bench. He would never truck with violence, but his ambivalence was as insidious as George's cast-iron bigotry, a subject in the old days for patrician table talk. "Keep them hostile," a powerful, landed neighbour had said with a bark-like chuckle, "but not too hostile." Now that this hostility had turned to rank hatred and daily murder, bigotry was no longer amusing. There seemed no solution. He moved towards the judges' stand. Alex was sitting on a low step of the platform, reading *The Belfast News Letter*, a cigar in his mouth; an ageing wrinkled primate in baggy suit, tartan shirt and horn-rimmed glasses, a hearing-aid clipped to his jacket. Harriet's ex-lover.

"Trouble, Nobby?"

"Nothing, where's Stuart?"

Alex pointed across the enclosure. Canon Plumm with rotund gravitas was talking to Professor Stuart Caldwell, the Canon gesticulating, Caldwell listening, the sun bright on his steel-framed glasses, a spare, almost boyish figure, clean and narrow as a sword. Alex folded the *News Letter* and thrust it into his jacket.

"It's the end, Nobby, the whole Show's folding ... matter of months, less."

"Saying that all your life Alex."

"This time it really is, 'course I've nothing to lose, you stand to lose a lot."

"Smallish crowd this year, not bad considering."

"In the old days I used to sit up trees at night with Basil watching out for Fenians or Germans ... they never came ... once I shot a rabbit ..."

Alex paused. Unlistening, the Colonel scanned the grounds as Alex asked, "Who's the enemy now, can you tell me that Nobby?"

"Harriet," the Colonel said quietly. "She's drinking a lot."

A man with a silver trophy walked past leading a Charolais bull with a rosette on its forehead. He saluted the Colonel who said, "Fine animal, Sam, well done."

"Foreign, Sir, the ould breeds is dying out."

"True."

They watched the great golden bull pad towards a loading ramp.

"Never understood the cattle business," Alex said. "Lost a fortune trying to."

The Colonel said again: "Harriet, Alex, she's drinking a lot."

Alex paused before saying: "She dislikes the American."

"Did she say so?"

"Can't you tell?"

Alex stood, brushing and blowing cigar ash from his jacket. "Imagine spending eternity with old Plumm!"

"With anyone ... can you speak to her?"

Alex shook his head. "She's out of reach ... and why die sober if you can afford to die drunk?"

"She's killing herself and you're facetious!"

"People get drunk to forget they're alive Nobby; happiness is under ground."

The Colonel pondered this for a moment and said, with edge: "That's heartless and rather stupid."

As the Colonel moved to join the Canon and Caldwell, Alex muttered to himself: "Suppose it is ... but then I'm bankrupt every way."

He took out another cigar and lit it. A group of farmers near by smiled indulgently. They could not hear what Alex muttered as he lit his cigar, but they knew he was Alex Boyd-Crawford, an oddity, something of a drinker and womaniser, a wise fool who would probably be the last of the Boyd-Crawfords, his estate depleted, a widower, his only son a drop-out, inheritor of one of the oldest names in Ulster.

Alex looked at his pocket-watch and muttered: "Show's folding, time for a drink."

He moved towards the marquee to extract Harriet without fuss.

"That," he muttered, "is one thing I can do better than Nobby."

LEONARD HAD DRIVEN about five miles on winding by-roads, through rolling drumlin countryside, up a dirt lane with high hedges to the front of a small two-storeyed farmhouse, painted tin over thatch, a byre adjoining, and beside it a small square concrete house with a rain-water tank above. There was a blue Cortina parked in an empty turf-shed.

"Where is this?" Lynam said.

"Mid-Monaghan. Townland of Drumgrone."

"Is there a bathroom?"

He pointed to the small concrete building and said: "A jacks."

"Can I wash?"

"There's a tap in the back yard."

She hesitated. Leonard added: "There's a river at the bottom of the garden."

"When do we leave?"

He looked at his wrist-watch: "Eight-thirty."

Leonard left her, went into the kitchen and directed his voice to someone behind the *Northern Standard*. "Where are the boys?"

From behind the *Northern Standard* a voice said: "Watching with Mother."

"We have a guest Jack."

"Yes?"

The paper did not come down.

"She'll be at the river in five minutes or less . . . keep her in sight and stay out of sight."

"She?"

"I'll tell you later; go out the back."

Jack Gallagher went out the scullery door, round behind the barn, and keeping to the fields walked alongside the wild garden.

Lynam went to the concrete toilet, then round to a tap dripping into a sandstone trough. A scullery window looked directly out. She left the yard walking through the haggard, past an empty haybarn into an overgrown garden, dense with nettles, docks, and some kind of wild rhubarb, rank and gross-smelling, that reached the lower branches of a dozen tortured apple trees.

There was a trodden path from house to river. She could hear water. The bank was steeper than she expected, bracken fronds fringing both sides at the roots of alder, ash and thorn. Water flowed clear over the rust-coloured bed. She sat on a dry stone by the edge of the water, took out a small wash-bag, mirror and make-up. Wet from tension, the cool air felt good. When she took off her blouse she noticed damp sweat patches, and realised she was more frightened now than she had been on the silent journey from Dublin. In an hour or less she would be facing, maybe talking with, those two people she had seen in the show-ground, and very possibly present when they were shot. Round a table or from a platform it was easy to talk and propagate the merits of violence as she had done for two years. Different now that it had prowled to her side, the bloody mid-wife of regeneration, a ruthless animal with dripping mouth and glassy merciless eyes. She took off her sandals, put her feet and hands in the water. In the snug of a bar in Dorset Street, when she had told Burke how she had ended the pregnancy, the gravel-voiced arbiter of life and death was so stunned he could scarcely reply.

"Why do that?" he had asked.

"It had no future."

"Why that?" he had repeated almost stupidly.

Was he so puerile that he saw her as a mere seed bed for his image? Why now without warning had he drafted her to possible martyrdom under Leonard? Pressures from others on the Army Council who disliked her bluntness? His wife's threat of suicide, or simply a cold, subtle move? Leonard, as yet publicly unknown, was privately spoken of North and South with a respect approaching awe which Burke must have noticed. And why had she joined? She tried to recall now her student impatience, bordering on hatred, for the congenital Irish condition, drunken meaningless talk breeding more drunken meaningless talk; an inability to think clearly and act coldly, "like the British" Burke said with irony. Once in, men who seemed complex became commonplace creatures jostling for power, a mix of waffling left-wingers, and old-fashioned Catholics led by Burke, who believed, she was certain, in nothing much but power for himself.

What now, sitting on a stone at a river's edge in Co.

Monaghan, did she believe on this August evening? Aloud to the water she said: "I don't know."

Before Birmingham she could have walked across this river through a series of hump-backed fields to the nearest village, 'phoned a taxi, and caught the Larne ferry to oblivion, like others unsure, frightened, or disillusioned.

Somewhere up the river she heard the liquid bleat of a curlew. The gable of her grandmother's house faced the sea. At night the curlews swept up the stony inlet past Coolfada to Dungarvan. Coolfada, thatched roof roped against storm, mud floor, white-wash gone brown, smoke-yellowed glass, hens, dogs, cats, meal bags, a Pierce bellows and the leather-faced old woman, blood of her blood muttering gaelic crossly to the animals, soda bread and sweet tea from a tin porringer in the morning, at night deep sleep in a settle bed in sheets stitched from flour bags, and God was the tide and all things related; people, fields, sea, sky, life and death, the immemorial land of childhood; lost.

It called again nearer. She looked up into the lowering sun as it winged closer. When she looked back to the river there was something floating downstream; rushes? a Moses' basket? The curlew wheeled calling again overhead and she thought "I'm hallucinating". Then she saw clearly a fawn shopping bag in rush-work design. It drifted past spinning in the shallows and on into a deep pool round the bend; plastic, illusive, childless. She had sacrificed the blood of her blood for what? A dream? Nothing, she thought, as fusty and narrow as nationalism or the dead sentimental drag of Coolfada. "No," she said aloud. She had chosen freely the waking nightmare of action, the comradeship of men whose vivid words, aims and violence seemed more attractive, honest and hopeful than the hollow crafty manoeuvrings of politicians like her father grinding out their mean, greedy lives towards anonymous death. For these reasons and others complex and unclear she had joined. Trapped now, frightened and betrayed, it was weak to say, "I don't know", but thinking ahead she was not only sickened by violence but terrified at the idea of staring in its awful face. "Oh God", she muttered, but knowing she did not believe in God she accepted now her cowardice as natural. No option; she had chosen: so be it.

Dressed, she felt cool and fresh. She scrutinised her face in the small mirror. Who stared back? If she could fully understand the mind behind that mask she might begin to understand others a little and the world.

As she made up her face she became suddenly aware of something, a presence? She looked around sharply. Thirty yards downstream a young man was sitting at the edge of the river, his head just visible above the grass and bracken, a white fish-belly face that often goes with vivid red hair, no Monaghan farm boy. He was smiling and the effect was both attractive and repellent. She put the mirror away in her handbag, anger growing. How long had he been there? More shameful, more revealing that he should see her search in her mirror than see her wash. The soul more private than the body. Had he heard her speak aloud? He was moving towards her, still smiling, medium build, regulation jeans, polo, jerkin and desert boots.

"What are you grinning at?"

"Not much."

"Did Leonard send you to watch?"

"You sound Dublin."

"You sound pure Fermanagh."

"Derry, love, and you're shivering ... you'll catch your death."

"Some day, and you?"

He was amused by her anger. "Don't let on you're ashamed by a man's eyes; what do they call you?"

"La belle dame sans merci."

The smile evaporated slowly; she waited for him to speak.

"I'm Jack Gallagher and I've notched five men in four years, three Brits, one R.U.C., one U.D.R., blown up three barracks, and left over a hundred bombs all over this province and when I ask a civil question I expect a civil answer."

She smiled up at him and said:

"Je m'appelle Isabel Lynam, et je voudrais changer les choses telles qu'elles soient, sans des salopards comme toi, mais la cause a besoin de toi, comme les champs ont besoin du fumier des cochons."

There was something in his expression that seemed almost subtle. She out-stared him, sure of her ground, till he turned and walked away from the river into the blind garden. Insulting and stupid of Leonard to have her watched like that. She picked up her handbag, momentarily aware that anger was more tolerable than fear, and that both were more tolerable than despair.

When Gallagher came into the yard Leonard could tell that he was tense.

"If I'm pig dung," he said, "she's sparrow shit. Bella Lynam, Christ man you're close, you could have warned me ... why all the mystery... ?"

"You saw her?"

"And heard ... smiling in my face she called me thug in French, that means you too boy, all of us."

"I said to keep out of sight."

"I was down river, she turned and saw me ... is she with us tonight?"

Leonard nodded.

"She's suspect."

"We're all suspect."

When they heard Lynam padding up the yard Leonard put a forefinger to his lips and made a small gesture commanding silence. When she came round the gable of the concrete toilet her face was inscrutable. Leonard smiled uneasily.

"Bella this is Jack Gallagher."

"We've met," Gallagher said without looking up.

She looked directly at Gallagher and said: "Yes I know him."

Leonard opened the door of the house to let her in.

The kitchen was startling, green, white and gold boldly used on walls, ceiling and lino, gleaming formica-top table, chrome kitchen chairs with leatherette seats. Above the stove an enormous oleograph of the Sacred Heart, between a butcher's calendar and the two Johns, Kennedy and Roncali, framed in smiling profile. All other available shelf and wall space was taken up with clocks, grandmother, grandfather, a dozen wall clocks, wag-o-the-walls, cuckoo clocks, shelves of ticking alarm and marble, clocks from railway stations and reading rooms, and one very impressive piece cast in iron from a big house yard or stable. The room itself seemed a clicking mechanism. As she took this in she heard Leonard say:

"Pacelli."

"Sorry?" she questioned.

Leonard repeated:

"Pacelli."

"Pius the thirteenth," Gallagher said.

A smallish youth approached her, a long almost monk-like face under crow black hair, with guileless eyes. A gunman? Incredulous, she took his hand as Leonard introduced her.

"Isabel Lynam."

"Bella," she said.

"We've heard plenty about you," Pacelli said. The voice had a sharp Monaghan edge, and the smile was disconcerting, both mocking and reassuring; he was older than he appeared.

"Pacelli what?" she asked.

"McAleer," he said.

"Touched like all the Monaghan McAleers," Gallagher said.

"He manes we believe in God, he lets on he doesn't."

A replica of Pacelli came round the staircase and Pacelli said: "This is Pascal the brother ... Bella Lynam."

As she shook hands she wondered if they were twins.

"How can I tell you apart?" she asked.

"Pascal has a bigger pendulum," Gallagher said.

Leonard smiled and Pascal said: "Jack's full of crack."

"But sour like a crab."

"Pay no heed."

"Pass no remarks."

"It's the kind of him."

"He can't help it."

"You'll get used to that," Gallagher said. "One goes tick the other goes tock."

Pascal pointed a forefinger at Gallagher, cocked up his thumb, closed one eye and said: "You'll mock once too often boy."

"I leave that to God," Gallagher said.

There was a short silence. It was clear to Lynam that the McAleer brothers did not approve of Gallagher's blasphemy. Seeing Gallagher close she noticed that his eyes were green, the whites blood-shot. His presence conveyed a tension you could almost touch. Because she knew he was a killer and enjoyed killing? Then Pascal said:

"You come on the express Bella?"

"By car."

Pacelli smiled:

"The Boyne at slane, ardee in rain
North to Carrickmacross
It's there the fields stare back and say
Eternity will be no loss

"What do you think of our little hills?"

"Pleasing."

"General Owen Roe marched through this townland in 1646."

"He did?"

"Retreated half dead from syphilis," Gallagher muttered.

"From what?" Pascal asked.

"Camp fever," Leonard said.

"Lovers' plague, Pascal ... won't bother you," Gallagher explained.

"What's he at Martin?" Pacelli asked.

Leonard shrugged. "We betray ourselves and are betrayed, and so we've lost time and again."

"*Not* what I meant," Gallagher said.... "Owen Roe tried and lost ... we'll win or die trying."

"Fair enough," Pascal said.

"I'm with you there," Pacelli added.

Gallagher looked at Lynam. "What do you say Mademoiselle?"

For five seconds Lynam stared back, before saying: "Little men who sneer at giants are ludicrous."

Leonard turned away so that Gallagher would not see him smile. Pascal aware of increasing tension intervened backed by Pacelli.

"The Mammy wants to meet you."

"She's above in the bed."

"An invalid."

"Bed-ridden this five years, arthritis and a dose of other things."

"She'll tell you herself."

"Likes to talk."

Leonard indicated to Lynam that she would have to do as requested. She followed Pascal across the gleaming green lino then up the narrow staircase. He opened a bedroom door.

"Bella Lynam from Dublin, Mammy, you've heerd tell of her."

A deep woman's voice uttered something in the room. Pascal smiled as she went in, closing himself out. Mrs McAleer was enormous, an Irish Queen Victoria, with De Valera's nose and Churchill's mouth, all chin and breast, her stomach making a tent of the patchwork quilt, plaited hair bunned up behind, and lenses so powerful that her eyes peered out in huge and permanent astonishment. She looked as though she could deliver Pascal and Pacelli fully grown. As Lynam approached Mrs McAleer held out a plump, regal hand. Lynam took it. It was clammy, the arthritic fingers rigid. The room had a personal fishy smell, mixed with Lysol and deodorant. Above a bedside commode a frail madonna stared upwards in tears, her heart transfixed by a sword. Beside the madonna, a calendar print of Padraig Pearse, his head in a halo of flames. Underneath someone had printed in red biro, his poem, "The Mother". Mrs McAleer said:

"You don't look twenty, I thought you'd be older."

"I feel like a thousand."

"You'll be with them tonight?"

"Yes."

"Are you afraid daughter?"

"Of course."

"It's a joy we can still breed your likes."

The fishmonger smell was oppressive. Lynam moved to a partially opened window and looked at the August landscape and the evening. Mrs McAleer patted the patchwork quilt and said:

"You can sit here by me."

"The view is beautiful," Lynam said.

"It is, it is, a wonder and a pity when you think of the men and women who died for them crooked hedges, ditches and lanes, the blood, the hunger, the burials, the old sorrow. I've suffered too all my life. Hughie my husband, that's him in the snap, used to say to me, 'Listen Rosie don't argue with God's will, he knows best,' a religious man, a feeling man, couldn't get doctors enough for me, London, Belfast, Dublin, no solution. They got him in '57 with a gun near Armagh, tortured and locked him away five years, then let him out to die. In this his deathbed he said to the boys, 'I'm broke lads, finished, but you have a score to settle,' and them only half reared, and me half crippled. Sometimes I think life's a bigger tragedy nor death. The Dublin Doctor Fagan said to me 'Mrs McAleer,' he said, 'there's nothing for it only aspirins and patience.' To myself I thought, 'Patience unto death'."

She paused to take a breath and change gear. "What do you think of my boys, daughter?"

"They seem nice."

"Small, like Hugh, but big hearts and clean living, and they've got nerve, don't smoke, don't drink, don't interfere with girls like that Gallagher, and they can take down any clock in the world and put it up again, and bombs... ! not a one in this country to touch them ... Mr Burke told me himself, 'You should be proud Mrs McAleer, proud, they'll get their reward and so will you.' Every day I thank God for my three green fields and my two brave sons."

She sighed. Lynam was about to say something when Mrs McAleer continued:

"I was once a slip of a girl like you would you believe that? And look at me now. Only for my two boys I'd be lost entirely, and I could lose them any time, some day, some night, like tonight, they'll go off, and the neighbour woman that cares me will come in some morning and say: 'I'm afeered Mrs McAleer I've bad news for you,' and I'll say: 'My boys is it, both?' And she'll nod."

Mrs McAleer bowed her head and quoted:

"Lord thou art hard on mothers,
We suffer in their coming and their going,

And though I grudge them not, I weary, weary
Of the long sorrow, and yet I have my joy,
My sons were faithful and they fought."

Mrs McAleer looked up. "I wouldn't be the first nor the last, it's the price of freedom; you're too young to understand the dread, your own flesh and blood dead in the cold earth."

"I understand."

"Young girls like you shouldn't be in danger ... war is men's work, if them Brits or black Protestants got hands on you, you'd never stand up to them ... what made you join, daughter?"

"That you wouldn't understand."

"Why not?"

"Because ..." Lynam paused, aware of the great devouring eyes, and said: "I don't understand myself."

"To free Ireland, it's simple."

"For what?"

"Us."

"From what?"

"Them."

"We are them ... now."

The blancmange cheeks trembled till the mouth uttered: "Never ... despise us, always did, always will."

From the window Lynam saw Gallagher cross the yard and place a canvas bag in the boot of the blue Cortina. She said quietly: "We died long ago with our language."

"What are you saying girl?"

"Win or lose nothing changes, because men don't nor women ... even the blind know that light leads on to darkness."

In the silence that followed, they could hear the ticking of innumerable clocks from the kitchen below. Mrs McAleer opened her mouth to say something, hesitated, then said, almost tenderly:

"You sound honest, do you pray daughter?"

"When I'm frightened."

"Do you believe in God?"

"Not yours."

"Jesus Christ?"

"Not yours."

The great face darkened again. On the edge of anger she said loudly. "There's only one Jesus Christ."

"Dozens Mrs Mac., and they hate each other."

There was a heavy silence punctuated by a sudden storm of cuckoo clocks and a dozen reverberating gongs in the kitchen.

"Are you a Communist, child?"

"I'm twenty-three. Arts Graduate, only child of Willie Lynam, Publican, Dáil Deputy and drunkard, separated from his wife, my mother, who devotes herself to poodles and Jesuits, and soon I will be in jail, exiled or dead."

Lynam paused and turned from the window. "What I am or think doesn't matter, but I'm glad we've met."

In silence Mrs McAleer pointed a crooked finger to a chest of drawers facing the bed.

"Left-hand drawer, open it."

Lynam did as she was asked. There was a cardboard box, a large plastic bottle and dozens of empty aspirin bottles filled with transparent liquid.

"Open the box."

Lynam took off the cardboard lid and saw a hoard of miraculous medals and chains.

"Take one and a small bottle."

Lynam felt absurd but knew refusal would give serious offence.

"Here daughter ... sit."

Mrs McAleer put the medal over Lynam's head and poked it under her blouse. Lynam slipped the aspirin bottle into her bag.

"You know what that is?"

"Holy water?"

"Better again, Lourdes water; she believes in you girl, and you mind that."

Mrs McAleer was holding her with a crab-like grip between rigid thumb and forefinger. Close up the two great floating eyes in that flaccid face had the impact of a Hogarth cartoon.

"Always wanted a daughter ... if I had one she wouldn't be troubled like you ... too much learnin' is the ruination of the world; all a body needs is faith in God, his Blessed Mother, faith in your people and faith in your country."

"Goodbye Mrs McAleer."

"God go with you child."

Lynam closed the door quietly and stood dazed in

the narrow upstairs hall. Mrs McAleer was a rural, republican edition of her genteel mother who fed anzaks and coffee to rotating Jesuits in return for vapid spiritual consolation. In every part of this island she had met men and women unreal beyond description. A race of inbred lunatics? Sometimes it seemed frighteningly like that.

She could hear Leonard talking below. When she rounded the bottom of the staircase he had his finger on a map or drawing. As she moved towards the table Gallagher came in the front door his cold face fixed in amused contempt. Without irony Pascal asked:

"You got your medal Bella?"

"Yes."

And Pacelli added: "Your wee bottle?"

Lynam nodded.

"Pre-war," Gallagher said. "Drink it and you'll get typhoid."

Pascal and Pacelli said almost together:

"Don't mind him."

"He's bred that way."

Gallagher smiled and said: "Tick tock, tick tock."

"Can we keep to this?" Leonard asked, his finger on a drawing. To Lynam he added: "You'll be with me, I'll gen you up on the way."

"Can I come and watch?" Gallagher asked.

For a moment it seemed as though Leonard would reply. It was Pacelli who spoke. "No call for talk like that."

"Like what?"

"Bad talk," Pacelli said.

"What the fuck did I say?"

Lynam moved away. In the silence that followed she read the legend on a butcher's calendar her back to the table. Pascal said:

"That's too much, no man should talk like that fornenct wemen."

"She doesn't give a shit about you boy, me, any of us."

"You can tell?" Leonard asked.

"I can tell," Gallagher said.

Her back to them Lynam said: "Let him fuck all he likes if it makes him feel manly."

"Not you," Gallagher said. "I don't pick over garbage."

The McAleer brothers were very uncomfortable. Leonard said quietly: "Jack please."

Lynam looked around. Leonard was white. A nerve twitched under his blind eye. She looked at the green lino aware of a sudden release of adrenalin. As always when tense she smiled. In the silence that followed the clocks seemed suddenly hysterical. Without opening his mouth Gallagher said:

"Bloody women, muck everything."

Leonard was aware that this was mostly his fault. Burke's cryptic coded note had advised him to watch her. The river thing was unfortunate. Either of the McAleers would have been more discreet, and Gallagher would have been more careful had he known who she was. To Gallagher all females were for screwing in ditches or cars. He boasted his prowess as lover and killer, how the girls whimpered, how his targets spun, stumbled and fell, date, street, and townland, all carefully reported back to Dublin: History. An epileptic, a sick aura of success hung about him, the black flag of violence and death. In the further silence Leonard looked from face to face, Gallagher's rigid, the McAleer brothers' aware of unseemliness. Lynam kept her head bowed. Was she smiling? With emphasis now he said:

"That's it."

"Come off it Martin."

Gallagher pointed a trigger finger at Lynam. "We know about her, Bella Donna, Burke calls her, she's poisonous, maybe Special Branch, Dublin or London, both the one ... you're doing the Belfast gent and she's laughing at you ... all of us ... look at her, we're a joke."

They all looked at Lynam. She lifted her head and stared back, her face indecipherable. Leonard paused for control. As he was about to speak a bell sounded upstairs.

"Mother Lourdes on the line," Gallagher said.

Both McAleers moved for the staircase. Leonard looked at his watch.

"Five minutes, boys, make your farewells...." To Gallagher he said: "You'd better say your bit and be done with this."

Gallagher said: "Thios ansin ag an abhainn thug tu

cailleach orm sul a rachaimid ait ar bit anois gabhfaidh tu mo leath sgeala."*

Lynam was startled. In the silence which followed a faint colour came into her narrow cheek bones. She said, nodding towards Leonard: "I was angry with him not you."

"Mea culpa, it was stupid of me."

"I'll drink to that," Gallagher said, and moved towards a cupboard beside the range. He took out a bottle of Powers Gold Label and half-filled three plain tumblers. He topped up with water from a jug, handed a glass to Leonard and Lynam, raised his own and said:

"To Ireland free."

"Whatever that means," Lynam muttered.

Gallagher lowered his tumbler. "From the centre to the sea, girl, that's what it means." He paused, looking intently into her face, and said: "And no deals, no compromise ever, no Catholic gents on horseback telling us what to think, no Murphys in a wig locking us away because they're afraid, no po-faced Prods whipping us for white nigger trash, no smug clergy hiding behind props and property, and whining about violence, no jet-set, pin-stripes buying up half the country; that's what it means Lynam." He jiggled his glass. "And death to all traitors ... you'll drink to that? ..."

"I'll drink to that."

"You believe it?"

* "Down at the river you called me a thug ... before we go anywhere you'll apologise."

"I'll drink to it."

She was startled, not so much by what he said but by the articulate intensity, the twisting mouth and blood-shot eyes, the low key fury as words came jerking out with barely controlled violence.... Had she misjudged him at the river as a boastful moron? This he was, but more. Could Leonard, anyone, control such a creature. The cold whiskey burned its way down, spreading a warm blurring numbness in her empty stomach. I'll be drunk in five minutes she thought, maybe dead by Monday. Gallagher added now:

"And success to the job."

"I'll be big," Leonard said, raising his glass and lowering his voice. "The world," he said, "and the socialist future."

"Does it have one?" Lynam asked.

"Can you let nothing by?" Gallagher asked.

"What the fight's about partly," Leonard intervened.

They drank and Gallagher looked at Lynam. "Now your dream?"

There was quite a pause till she said with an odd smile: "Life and death."

They hesitated.

"Whose death?" Gallagher asked.

"Peace," she said.

"That's better," Leonard said, and realised that she knew clearly as he did what they were venturing.... Two Army Council meetings had been, he was told, entirely taken up with "The Inver Move". The first vote went against, the second in favour. He had spent three long days and sleepless nights being briefed in Dublin. At the time Burke had said that he might send extra help, but had given him no hint that it would be Lynam. Since then Leonard had thought of nothing else night and day, trying to justify in advance, to cancel fear and doubt. The wealth and privilege of the Armstrongs in these islands and Europe had been gained by force and fraud, sanctioned and maintained by Church and Law for centuries. This he told himself again and again. If London refused to negotiate they would have to kill and be killed. The clamorous condemnations that would follow were nothing; they would be at peace. He had shot one soldier near Strabane two years ago and one bomb he had placed had killed a mother and child. It was painful to see images in newspapers and read accounts. Sometimes he heard screaming in his sleep and woke sweating. Unlike Gallagher he had never seen, nor wanted to, the face of a victim. This time they would be face to face in one room for eighteen hours or more. As the McAleers came down the staircase Leonard asked:

"Time?"

Pascal and Pacelli looked at their wrist-watches, smiled at the clocks round the walls and said:

"Eight twenty-five."

"Dead on."

Gallagher and Leonard adjusted their watches fractionally and Leonard said: "We leave in five minutes."

Pascal and Pacelli came up to Leonard and shook his hand in solemn ritual. They then turned to Lynam.

She was about to offer her hand when Pascal kissed her on one cheek, Pacelli on the other. Both had the same joyous, guileful smiles, at variance with their guileless eyes. Gallagher watched them go out the door, followed, turned and said:

"Slán."

"Slán," Leonard and Lynam said simultaneously.

"Have they killed?" she asked.

"Yes."

"Both?"

"Yes."

"And you?"

"Yes."

"All but me."

"You might have to."

"I know."

"You have a weapon?"

"No."

Leonard put his glass down. She noticed he had scarcely touched it. He went to the built-in cupboard where Gallagher had found the whiskey, took out two shelves, removed a loose board from the back and put his hand into a cavity. He took out a small pistol.

As he explained how it worked his voice seemed far away. She could see his scarred thumb pressing the catch, his forefinger curling round the trigger: then words: "Dead simple, safety catch, gentle pressure, flick this here, can't miss, hold the shooting wrist with your hand, like this." Gallagher's measure of whiskey seemed to heighten the gleaming phallic awfulness in Leonard's hands. He undid the catch of her bag, and thrust in the pistol. If he had unzipped his fly, peeled off a used condom and dropped it in her bag, she would have been less shocked. He was aware of her silence.

"All right?"

"Fine."

As he held the front door open he called out: "Monday night late Mrs Mac."

The deep voice above sent down a sepulchral blessing.

The Cortina went first, Pascal driving, Gallagher in front, Pacelli in the back. After ten minutes scudding along a by-road into the gathering dusk they passed a sign which said: "UNAPPROVED ROAD".

From the back seat Pacelli grinned and gave the thumbs up sign. Leonard nodded and thumbed back at him.

"This is it," he said.

Lynam did not answer. After a mile she said: "We're dead."

"Every time I think that and I'm still alive."

"This is different."

"More difficult ... if it wasn't it wouldn't be worth doing."

"Suppose we're stopped on the way by Police or Army?"

"We won't be."

"Suppose?"

"This road's checked out, and all by-roads."

"How?"

"Friends."

The Cortina slowed, turned left up a by-road; as Leonard slowed to follow he said: "Clumsy ... the river thing, I'm sorry."

Lynam said nothing for a minute, then asked: "Where did he get French?"

"Brittany, Breton Freedom Fighter."

"Will he do what you say?"

"Jack? I think so."

"Think?"

"I'm sure."

"He's paranoid, schizoid."

"Epileptic."

"I could sense something, the sick colour and the raving."

"If it comes to killing he won't waste words."

"Or pity?"

"No," Leonard said, "he's dedicated and deadly."

"What did Burke tell you?"

"If it was serious you wouldn't be here."

"Tell me."

Leonard hesitated before saying: "Anyone who can wreck two marriages and arrange three press leaks in one year should be in advertising or a brothel."

"He's lying ... reptile."

"All of us, if you believe the Press, Churches and politicians."

In a few sentences Leonard outlined what she would have to do. He asked if she was clear. She said yes she was. They were now in forest twilight away from the small drumlin fields with their ditches of thorn and thwarted ash. They sped past a limestone baronial gate-lodge with conifers crowding and stretching back into the embracing dark. A hundred yards further on there was an obelisk in a circular clearing, its base engraved in gold lettering. Leonard said, nodding at it:

"The dead of two world wars."

"Is this Inver?"

Leonard nodded. The Cortina had stopped a hundred yards from the monument where the high estate wall had been smashed by a falling tree. Gallagher and Pascal had gone through. Pacelli took the canvas bag from the boot and followed. Leonard drew in behind the Cortina and cut his engine. As Lynam stepped over the rubble of the wall she saw below a long stretch of lake and meadowland and, beyond the lake, bunched in trees and shrubbery, the outline of a tall Tudor house.

MILLICENT LEFT THE tray on the pantry table, plugged in the coffee percolator and watched her father decanting port, waiting for him to say something.

"I've spoken to her."

"When?"

"Before dinner."

The Colonel inserted a cork firmly into the empty bottle of port as his daughter said: "Her blouse is buttoned the wrong way, and out at the back, and she's been like a zombie all through dinner."

"Worse when she talks."

"It's awful to say this, father, but I'll leave on Monday if she doesn't ... I can understand today at the Show, but other days where does she get it?"

"The staff are 'loyal'."

"Why is she so unhappy?"

"Why does winter come?"

"She fell in the marquee when Alex went to ..."

"Yes I heard."

"Such a mockery of a man."

"He's kindly, reads a lot, they share that."

"Don't you care?"

The Colonel had moved towards the heavy, panelled self-closing door that gave to the living-room. If he said yes it would be short of honest. No, and it would seem that he did not love or cherish his wife, her mother, when in truth he had connived at the affair through guilt. He looked at the decanter of port and said:

"Yes and no."

"That's not an answer."

"The best I can give."

Because they were only six the hunting table was opened before the Adam grate in the long high-ceilinged living-room cleared now except for two ash-trays, port glasses, and some cut-glass tumblers. Harriet was sitting at the head of the table facing the high, wide, bay window that looked south-west across the lake. All through dinner she had been watching a dark red sun go down behind the forest lands of Inver and Shannock, leaving the lake a blooded gash in the quiet landscape. Now, as she watched, the blood congealed to a blackish, navy-blue, as lake, field and forest merged into night.

Caldwell had been talking and getting attention through dinner. Harriet lit her last cigarette watching the moving lips, hating the intelligent blue eyes behind those steel frames, the sickening drawl, the elegant brown safari-type jacket, and creamy silk shirt that seemed to blend with his feminine skin. Alex was nodding, bored, she thought. Canon Plumm seemed attentive. Suddenly the Canon's face broadened. He gave a short avuncular laugh. Caldwell smiling touched the tip of his fine-boned nose with a long left forefinger. Harriet noticed the perfectly groomed nails. Some rhyming joke? She had missed it. In the momentary pause that followed she said with unusual loudness:

"Very stupid of me but I seem to have missed the point."

The Colonel was at the other end of the table. As he sat and placed the decanter of port he said with quiet hardness: "Possibly you weren't listening my love."

Caldwell said: "It's nothing."

"But Canon Plumm laughed." Harriet said. "It must be amusing."

There was a longer pause. Harriet looked from face to face and then began:

"Sitting snugly at his fire William Wordsworth said to Charles Lamb, 'I could write plays like Shakespeare if I'd a mind to,' and Lamb replied, 'Nothing lacking Willie, but the mind'."

Alex Boyd-Crawford smiled; he had heard it before. No one else responded. Harriet went on:

"Oscar Wilde envied that reply, did you know that Professor?"

"I did not."

"Shy man Lamb, devoted to his sister, charming essays."

Harriet could see the knuckles of her husband's hands go white as both fists closed. Surely he wasn't going to bang the table? She kept her eyes down and heard Caldwell say:

"More sick than funny I suppose."

"What?" Harriet asked.

Canon Plumm explained. "Professor Caldwell was

telling us about some grave inscriptions in eighteenth-century Virginia."

"Which Virginia?"

"United States."

"Grave inscriptions?"

"Yes."

"Funny ones, Professor?"

"Odd ones," Caldwell said.

"In our graveyard here," Canon Plumm ventured, when Harriet cut in suddenly.

"Hideous subject, utterly."

She searched the ornate Italian frieze for a word, found it and uttered emphatically:

"Horrendous ... numbing ... if you ponder it ... thy kingdom dumb ... terrifying...." She paused. "But life itself, now there's true comedy, because people do the strangest, the most anguish-making, cruelly funny things ... friends, neighbours, nations ... when I think of the things we all do to each other in the course of living, in the mill of history, I laugh and laugh till the tears come."

Harriet bowed her head. She was trembling, forgot what she was saying and why, aware only that Milly had placed a tray with coffee cups and percolator on the table and was now sitting down.

"What was I saying Alex?"

"Something about life dear."

"Ah yes, some burial joke that Dr Caldwell made.... I missed the point, and that is a defect, not to respond to the niceties of civilised necrophilia."

The Colonel said coldly: "Harriet."

"Yes my love?"

"Would you like to pour coffee?"

"I'll pour," Millicent said.

They watched as she poured, each responding when she asked about sugar and cream.

"Some graves," Alex said vaguely, "are self-dug."

"Indeed," the Colonel said, looking directly at his wife. Behind those eyes, she thought, a mind foreign as his locked study. The charm was for others, that tilt of the head as though he could listen for ever. Long since he had stopped hearing unless she screamed. What had she loved or thought she loved? The soldierly bearing, the graceful manners, the family accumulations, in Tudor mellowness. He knew about everything in the house, who bought it, where, when, why, how much it was insured for. Yes. He understood about insurance. "Any policy, Nobby, for a withering heart?" He had smiled that night as though she had asked a silly question, the smile he used when talking with her gifted unpredictable father whose money had helped finance the expensive yards, the milking merry-go-round, the yards full of cows and bawling bullocks. Some time near dawn she had smashed three plates of value against the door of his study. He did not refer to the gesture at the time or since. The armour of infinite politeness, behind it something callous; inhuman.

Aloud she said, "Inhuman."

No one seemed to hear. The talk now had shifted to employment, the E.E.C. and agriculture. Agriculture.

His real devotion since the war; his hobbies, military and local history: "The Armstrongs in Ulster: The intruders who contributed."

In the functions room of an Armagh hotel his paper was well received by the Clogher Historical Society, Catholics and Protestants, mostly teachers and clergy. She had read it in advance and thought it dull and tendentious. When he spoke it standing upright in that warm level voice, it sounded humane, conscientious, liberal. Everyone likes him for some reason, she thought . . . perhaps I'm jealous. . . . Yes. All that correspondence with Denis Brogan which she had resented till they met at Cambridge, an Irish-Scot professor, with a port-wine face, startling white hair, and a mind so complex and comprehensive that his tongue stumbled after, a soul more alive to poetry and philosophy, than the brutal facts and farce of war. In comparison Caldwell was an intellectual eunuch, a beautiful, polished New England eunuch. She was aware now that they were all looking at Alex. Watching his pursed mouth she forced herself to understand what he was saying. He paused, shrugged and continued:

"We never employed Papists, family tradition, they all cheat, lie and thieve, dirty, careless, superstitious, stupid; when you hear this from the nursery onwards, right or wrong it tends to stick."

"Fact, Sir," Canon Plumm said gravely. "They've a lower I.Q. than Negroes, an American professor has proven this, am I right Dr Caldwell?"

Caldwell considered a moment and said: "That study is controversial, Canon."

"To the Irish, no one else; what they've done down there in sixty years is not in doubt, ruined Dublin, painted pillar boxes green, and produced more lunatics and alcoholics per square mile than any other country in the world. This is proven fact."

Harriet finished her glass of wine, wiped her mouth with a napkin.

"Did you not say, Milly, that this lovely county of ours has the worst housing problem in these islands?"

"It has," Millicent said.

"Papist housing you'll find," the Canon said, "won't avail of grants, they're shiftless and Rome's responsible."

"Rome?" Harriet asked.

The Canon smiled and shook his head patiently as he muttered: "Italy, Spain, Portugal, Latin America."

He opened his hands and pursed his lips. The target was so enormous he did not know quite where to aim. Suddenly he struck. "Take Plunkett, the rebel priest, hung as Crown traitor. This year they plan to canonise him."

He paused, staring from face to face. "Here their Bishops preach against violence while the Pope in Rome aligns himself with I.R.A. bombers and murderers."

He paused again. "This is not just mischievous; it's political, criminal."

There was an embarrassed pause, until Harriet said:

"We did burn Joan of Arc, Canon ... they made her a saint."

"Different."

"Is it? Of course I don't understand politics; Nobby does and Professor Caldwell is an expert. How does it strike you, Professor, as an outsider? Will we be shot in our beds, driven to the sea, what's your impression?"

"Do you want an answer?"

"I did ask a question."

"Unlikely ... implausible."

"Then what is plausible?"

Stuart Caldwell stirred his coffee for ten seconds, aware that no reply could please.

"I expect," he said quietly, "the British will leave in time, and North and South will patch up something in time, with or without a civil war ... impossible to say more."

Almost inaudibly Harriet muttered: "Profound."

Glacial, the Colonel asked: "You have some solution, dear?"

"No, but I did think the Canon just now sounded peasant as Paisley without the loudmouthed charm, and I don't trust his American professor I.Q. expert, or indeed anything from that glorious civilisation."

"Mother."

"You've got a degree dear, what did they teach you at Trinity? To keep silent when people talk nonsense?"

Harriet looked down the table at her husband. Centuries of arrogance in those bloodhound eyes that stared back from that long hawk-like face drained of colour, the iron grey head and clipped moustache fringing a heavy mouth. She looked away to the window across the lake.

The Colonel looked up at his wife who was avoiding his eyes. Last night she had fallen asleep at table. He had excused the staff and helped Milly serve dinner to eight people. Her performance this evening was a great deal more painful. Of course John Plumm was something of a bigot and a bore, but also well-meaning in his way, apart from being a very old friend. Stuart was much too sophisticated to respond to drunken petulance. Tomorrow when she half remembered what she had just said she would suffer. He felt both angry with her and sorry for her.

Harriet stood suddenly and walked with particular care towards the pantry door. In the continuing silence Alex said:

"Excellent coffee ... excellent."

"It is," Caldwell said.

The Colonel stood and said to Canon Plumm and Caldwell: "I'm sorry."

The Canon shook his head and mumbled something. Caldwell smiled and made a small gesture. The Colonel followed Harriet. She was standing at the sink with a large whiskey looking out at the August night. The Colonel approached quietly, held her wrist, took the glass from her hand and moved to the table. She watched with anger and disbelief as he poured the whiskey back into a newly-opened bottle of Haig then heard herself say:

"That was a stupid thing to do."

"You've been warned my love . . . you're killing yourself."

"I'm dead."

"Drunk, dear, and the trouble is you'll fall and crack your skull or crash the car."

"A blessed relief."

The Colonel looked at the label on the whiskey bottle and said: "Irish is cheaper than Scotch and better for making you drunk. If you get more . . ."

"A blessed relief, I said. And you will not humiliate me like this."

The Colonel watched, impassive, a seasoned politician pausing for an irrelevant heckler. Looking from the scrubbed deal table to her glazed brown eyes he said with growing edge:

"If you get more maudlin than you are now, insult guests like that, laugh hysterically at nothing, or jabber incomprehensible verse, I'll send for someone."

He had hinted before; now it had been said. She felt anger grow to a point of fury.

"Someone!"

"Qualified."

She turned her back and said to the window: "Get a medical plumber for me, Nobby, and I'll 'phone someone for you . . . also qualified."

There was a very long pause before the Colonel said: "What are you trying to say my love?"

"I can see through him with my eyes shut."

"Who?"

"Caldwell."

"You dislike him?"

"He makes me ill, I want him gone."

"You could have said so without all this."

The Colonel went back to the living-room. Harriet leaned against the pantry sink supporting herself with both hands. The table before her seemed momentarily a raft riding on a gentle swell. She closed her eyes aware that the door leading off the pantry to the kitchen corridor had opened quietly, or had she imagined it? She opened her eyes and saw a young man with blood red hair above a corpse white face. He was pointing a pistol at her. He waved her away from the sink. More incredulous than afraid she moved as directed towards the table and thought to herself: I'm dreaming. The young man locked the door, moved across the pantry, locked another door leading to the hall, went to the sink, pulled the shutters across the window, then the curtains, and pointed towards the door leading into the living-room. As she opened this green baize door she saw another young man, tall, with a black beard, standing with a pistol at the far end of the room, beside him a girl with a tense narrow face, and melancholy eyes. The girl had no weapon in her hand. The man with the beard spoke.

"No hardship intended if our request is met."

The red youth walked down the long room, pulled shutters across the bay window, then the heavy tapestry curtains, ensuring that there was no gap in the middle or at either side.

The family portraits round the walls looked calmly down on the upturned faces round the hunting table, each face expressing varying degrees of incomprehension and disbelief. The Tomkin clock on the high mantel ticked evenly in the stillness that followed Leonard's cryptic statement, beech logs hissed in the Adam fire-basket. Lynam looking from face to face was startled by a sudden shock of recognition: "No... ! Yes... ? Trinity... ? Armstrong... ? good Christ... !" They had shared French tutorials three years ago. She could see that the Armstrong girl could not believe the evidence of her own eyes. To Lynam she said:

"It is you?"

"Yes," Lynam said.

High in the great house they could hear shutters squealing on rusty hinges, the rasp of iron clasps, the twanging of six-inch nails being driven into doors, architraves, windows.

Leonard switched on the lights.

"How many?" the Colonel asked.

"Two more."

"How long will you keep us?"

"Tomorrow midday, unless they give us what we ask."

"And that is?"

"Three men from Long Kesh."

"And if not?"

"Bleak ... for all of us."

Gallagher approached and whispered, nodding

towards the table:

"Milord Secretary ... he's gone... !"

"We'll make these do."

"Bad start."

"Good omen."

Watching them the Colonel guessed the content and spoke:

"You know that what you're attempting is not just misguided, it's plain stupid."

The red-haired youth made a brief grimace. The man with the beard, obviously the leader, returned the Colonel's stare. His left eye was sunken in its socket, both heavy-lidded above a prow-like nose, the dense beard creating a mask-like effect. Having spoken, the Colonel now felt he had to act. He stood, not quite knowing what he intended, and moved towards Leonard. With scarcely a movement of lips a voice came from the beard with emphasis:

"No further."

The scarred forefinger of his left hand was pointing rigidly. The effect was more menacing than a pistol. Some instinct advised the Colonel that this man was professional and would kill without hesitation. He paused, looked at the decanter of port on the table and said:

"You expected my son-in-law here ... he's chairing a symposium at Queen's University. I would have thought you knew this—it was well publicised. You can't bargain with an old soldier, his family and a couple of friends—won't work. You'll have to kill us—

they'll kill you—and nothing whatever will have been gained but bad propaganda for you and more business for the undertakers, and God knows they're overworked in this Province.... Be sensible ... you can still leave."

"Your Army is notified," Leonard said. "On its way."

"If they don't get lost about Belturbet," Gallagher muttered.

"Dear God," Canon Plumm almost whispered.

"I think," the Colonel said, "that you should know this gentleman is an American professor."

Gallagher said: "He could be an Australian kangaroo."

Leonard nodded agreement. "He's here and stays till we decide ... otherwise, no hardship. The house will be sealed excepting the front door and hall, this room, the pantry and toilet off."

The Colonel said: "You know the house well."

"National Trust," Leonard said. "The plans are available and clear."

Harriet looked at her husband as the nailing continued above. "We're being entombed, Nobby, alive."

Milly said: "Mother, I think ..."

"We can talk, can we not?"

"All you like," Leonard said.

"Then I think we should introduce ourselves."

In the silence that followed Leonard said: "Our names don't matter."

"Ours do.... I am Harriet Armstrong and that is my

husband Norbert, beside him is Stuart Caldwell, a Professor of military history ... a subject indistinguishable from pornography in my view.... I read a lot of poetry ... Dylan Thomas mostly."

Milly said: "Mother this is not helpful."

Leonard said: "I'm quite interested."

"In mockery," Millicent said acidly.

"I said 'Quite'."

Harriet went on: "The Professor probably knows more about the I.R.A. than any of you people."

"I doubt it," Gallagher said.

"And this," she said, putting out her hand towards Alex, "is Alex Boyd-Crawford retired from ... what are you retired from Alex?"

"Everything," Alex said.

"But genial courtesy and warmth ... human warmth ... rare in this cold world ... and beside me this roundabout man is dear Canon Plumm, the Rector of Inver Church ... an expert on bee-keeping." She paused and smiled before adding: "And the machinations of the Vatican.... And my daughter Millicent, twenty-four years old ... married ..."

"Harriet you will stop talking now," the Colonel's voice cracked out in hard sharp command.

Harriet shrugged, picked up an empty cigarette carton, examined it, turned to Gallagher and asked: "Do you have a cigarette?"

Without answering Gallagher produced a packet with his free hand and flicked it on to the table.

"Thank you."

As Harriet lit a cigarette, Gallagher studied the six faces round the table, then moved away and began pacing the length of the room, pausing once or twice before family portraits, glancing into the great gilt mirror above the chimneypiece which framed the hostages round the table, now looking into each others' eyes like passengers aboard plane or ship when an engine bursts into flame, or a voice warns suddenly of serious emergency. The man with the beard, who was obviously the leader, seemed almost casual, talking in a low voice with the girl. The red youth seemed very tense and by far the most dangerous. Every now and then his pistol wrist gave an involuntary twitch like the tail of a caged tiger.

Watching him Lynam realised with slow horror that he would convey this tension till he had tasted blood. He wanted to kill or be killed, and she wondered if this, less manifest, was a hidden instinct in herself, in Leonard, in the McAleers. Then she saw the Colonel lean over the back of the American's chair and say something to his daughter who asked:

"Can I fetch some whiskey?"

"Where from?"

"The pantry."

Leonard nodded and said quietly to Lynam: "Go with her."

Millicent got up. Lynam followed and stood in the panelled pantry beside a Welsh dresser decked with Spode china, Wedgwood, oriental ware, and topped with an array of pewter mugs and containers. Millicent hunkered, reached into a corner cupboard and took out two bottles of Bushmills whiskey aware that Lynam was standing behind her. She straightened, turned, and said:

"When I heard your voice I knew ... Isabel Lynam?"

"Yes."

"Impassioned at debate I remember ... I listened then, I'll listen now."

"This is not a college debate, and I didn't know you lived here ... unfortunate."

"You're Provisional I.R.A.?"

"Obviously."

Millicent put the two bottles on the scrubbed deal table and dropped her voice: "Those two horrors inside ... with faces like that ... I can see them doing anything ... not you."

"One has three A levels and I find their faces less horrific than the painted ones round your walls."

"You'll kill me, my parents, friends, a churchman, in cold blood?"

Lynam did not answer.

"You can maim, cripple, blind the innocent ... for what?"

"You've never been colonised, you wouldn't understand."

"I can try, if you can explain."

The unafraid manner and arrogant voice seemed patronising. She had long flaxen hair, immaculate skin, and brown searching eyes, eloquent as her mother's but less vulnerable. Lynam felt suddenly docked by a hostile witness, a self-possessed, model girl with a modelled upper-class mind. Looking straight back she said:

"I don't have to."

"You can't ... you've had your student pub-crawls, your bedsit affairs, hitched about and got stoned, so now you're a graduate ... work's a bore, what next ... back-room politics with mindless killers ... a taste of terror before you die ... it's beyond contempt."

Lynam did not react and said after quite a pause: "You married?"

Surprised, Millicent glanced at her wedding ring: "I was to have our first child in January ... does that mean anything to you."

"Capricorn."

"What!?"

"Capricorn."

"I don't think you're quite human."

"Yesterday, Victoria Regina Magnifica gave five pounds for Irish famine relief and the same week five pounds to a British dog fund."

"Yesterday?"

"She's still alive ... when you stop killing us we'll stop killing you ... it's as simple as that."

"What have I ... we ... got to do with killing you?"

"Everything."

"You're not sane."

"Very, and human, and distressed about your child ... if there's anything I can do?"

The door came in and Gallagher was suddenly

standing in the pantry. He paused, looking from one girl to the other, walked between them picking up a cut glass tumbler from the table on his way to the sink. Millicent left. Gallagher tapped off three full glasses and drank them without pause and then held the tumbler up to the light.

"Eighteenth-century Waterford; Huguenot rubbish."

He dropped the tumbler: it shattered in the teak sink.

"A Protestant cultural victory ... nicked the Book of Kells too ... how goes it girl?"

"Fine."

He looked at her for a moment in silence and then said: "I like you Lynam."

"You don't and it's reciprocal."

Blinking oddly Gallagher ran his tongue round his upper lip and asked: "Why?"

"Boasting your kills; sickening."

"That a fact?"

Gallagher looked at her, his eyes moving slowly from her legs up her body to her face. "Contrary bitch ... you preach killing and puke on killers ... two-faced ... you're like your old man Lynam, a Republican fraud."

He moved towards the door, turned as he opened it and said: "One thing, Mise Eire nua,* a dodgy move ..." he flicked his pistol, "and I'll be watching.... I don't trust you."

When Gallagher had left Lynam said quietly: "Nor I, myself."

* The modern Kathleen ni Houlihan

Passing the table as Caldwell poured whiskey, Gallagher said: "Enjoy it, Sir."

"I'll try," Caldwell said.

Leonard had pulled an ornate chair into the shuttered bay window, a solitary audience, aware of murmurs and movement round the table, the faces imprinted on his mind by the initial exchange. As time passed he would get to know each face in more detail, and cold action if it had to come would be that much more awful. He was aware of tension in himself as he listened to the McAleers' hammering above, and imagined the guttural roar of pigs and Saracens which would arrive from Lisnaskea within fifteen minutes or less.

Now as he saw Gallagher come padding down the room he realised that he was glad to see him. He had argued strongly with Burke against taking him on this job pointing out that he was epileptic, and might prove unpredictable. "You'll be glad of him," Burke had said. Gallagher approached, leaned towards Leonard and said quietly:

"Heard Lynam say to the daughter 'if there's anythin' I can do'."

"They were at college together."

Gallagher stood alongside Leonard watching the table: "Smug ... look at them ... we should smash something ... make them dance on the table, face the wall with their arms out."

"Pointless Jack, relax."

"I will."

Without warning Gallagher moved from the bay window towards bookshelves on either side of the fire-place that went from floor to ceiling. He stood there for a minute or so reading titles. He then put his pistol on the high mantelpiece, took out a book and read aloud: *"The Un-finished War, by Eric Moore Ritchie."*

He opened the book and read from the fly leaf: "The drama of Anglo-German Conflict in Africa in relation to the future of the British Empire ... eight maps, published London, 1940 ... includes campaigns in East Africa, Cameroons and Togoland."

Gallagher paused and said: "Or: who owns the Nig Nogs, their nuts and their nickel."

He put back Eric Moore Ritchie took down another book and again read aloud: *"Pig Sticking or Hog Hunting, by Sir Robert Baden-Powell.* A complete account for sportsmen and others, published London, 1824."

Gallagher looked at the Colonel and asked: "Enoch's Great grand-daddy?"

He replaced Baden-Powell and said: "Nothing in our culture to match that ... makes you feel inferior ... humble ... we've a long way to go ... we bog, we pig-in-the-parlour Irish ... yes, Sir, a long way to go."

He picked up a nearby chair, moved towards the table and sat, placing the chair between the Colonel and Boyd-Crawford.

"Would you like to pour me a dram, Sir?"

"Of course," the Colonel said evenly.

The Colonel poured a generous measure.

"You buy Irish?"

"Northern Irish," Canon Plumm said.

"We know; they boast no natives near the mash, we have a long list of all such firms ... I'll not discriminate ... your good health."

Gallagher drank and said: "You're American Sir?"

"That is correct."

"Caldwell ... Fermanagh stock ... good planter name ... Nixon too ... great people ... must make you feel proud ... kinship with high office ... doing a book on the troubles, Professor?"

"Research."

"Into what?"

"Ulster under Elizabeth the First."

"The Virgin Queen in Ulster?"

"She didn't come here."

"That a fact. No virgin either, was she? ... but she could pick good butchers ... men with big swords ... big cannon balls ... still does ... nice day for killing ... that's what the Paras said in Derry ... Lizzie II's high-jumping men ... kill in Irish means Church ... cuill a wood ... darkness and death ... might teach you some Irish tonight ... a few sad songs ... we've got hundreds ... but this war is not merry ... it's ugly, very very ugly, and we'll keep it ugly till it's over."

Gallagher drained the rest of his whiskey and looked in silence from face to face.

"I like talking, but you don't like what I say ... it's the silence: I can tell ... but as the night goes on the atmosphere may improve ... we must hope for progress towards a general understanding of the underlying tensions that gulf our ancient cultures over seven centuries ... we've been under ... while you were lying."

Gallagher suddenly hacked a cross on the patina of the hunting table with the bead of his pistol. "The cross and the sword: the glory of Europe."

He then placed it sideways on the table and spun it with his forefinger. As it twirled he said to Caldwell: "This is what they do in your Westerns."

It stopped with the nozzle facing Alex Boyd-Crawford: "A fossil first!"

Gallagher took the hearing-aid clipped to Alex's handkerchief pocket and using it like a microphone asked loudly: "Do you think there's any hope for peace in our time Sir?"

Alex jerked, pulling out the earpiece as Gallagher's voice exploded in his left eardrum. With a sudden movement Gallagher whipped the hearing-aid from his jacket and smashed it on the hearth.

"Deaf anyway ... all of you ... you'll hear and listen before we quit."

Harriet broke the silence that followed: "I think he means it Nobby."

"Every word," Gallagher said.

Impassive the Colonel turned to Leonard: "Are you supposed to be in charge?"

Leonard did not reply and kept watching till he caught Gallagher's eye. Gallagher went to him and hunkered to listen.

"They'll be here soon."

"I can't sit."

"Then move around."

The door leading to the front hall opened. Pacelli McAleer's black head appeared. He grinned and came in, followed immediately by Pascal carrying a canvas bag. Pascal smiled at Leonard.

"That's it, all nailed, wired and locked."

Pacelli looked about the magnificent room with mock awe.

"Damn it, this is a powerful place."

"It's a palace, man, a palace."

"There's beds above big as a council kitchen."

"Sleep a whole fambley."

Both stared at a full length portrait of a Judge in wig and red gown, a parchment in his hand.

"Like a house'd nourish ghosts," Pascal said.

Pacelli grinned. "Every class but the Holy Ghost."

As Lynam came in from the pantry Pascal groped in the canvas bag and began issuing tear-gas masks. As Gallagher slipped one over his head, leaving it hang, he said:

"Christmas in June; thank you Santy; you're full of surprises."

Leonard pointed towards the pantry door and said: "Out there boys: three doors. Check them."

The McAleers left followed by Gallagher. As Lynam

moved to join Leonard she saw the hearing-aid smashed on the hearth.

"What provoked that?"

"Jack, tense like us ... and a bit hung over."

"The daughter's pregnant."

Leonard did not react.

"Can we let her go?"

Leonard nodded.

"Now?"

"Not yet.... How do you feel?"

"Scarified. What now?"

Leonard looked at his watch and said: "Forces from demi-paradise."

"How long?"

"They're late."

As he spoke they heard in the distance the heavy-engined growling of Saracens, jeeps, and pigs in convoy a mile off or less. Leonard stood and went to the deep recess of the doorway giving to the long hall. Lynam followed and stood beside him, her heart jumping as the growl increased to a deep-throated roar. Gallagher was back in the room sitting in the chair Leonard had left, his pistol levelled at the table.

"The Army of the Empire full of beans and bitters, I could smell them coming."

It was five minutes before the armoured wagons rolled up the long avenue to the wide front, scattering gravel, screeching to a standstill. Silence, then the sound of massive, steel-plated doors clanging shut, voices, cryptic orders, a search-light beaming through the glass panels of the tall front door. Lynam was shaking so badly she felt her legs would give. She whispered to Leonard:

"Martin."

"Yes."

It was the first time she had used his name.

"I can't."

"Can't what?"

She was in deep shadow beside him.

"Kill."

"Can you do the other?"

"I think so."

Leonard nodded and said: "On you go."

She moved from the terror of keeping still into the beam of the Army search-light. She unlocked and unbolted the front door and went out. As she walked down the wide granite steps she was aware of shadows behind the Saracens and jeeps, the search-light tilted slightly to follow her descent. Pausing at a flagged break in the stairway and shading her eyes against the militant light she flung her voice towards the dark massive shapes.

"I want to speak to the Commanding Officer."

"Over here," a Sandhurst voice from the right said.

"Here," she said, replying to the voice.

There seemed a thirty-second delay before she heard the crunching of footsteps coming towards her over gravel, then the briskness of leather boots on stone. Then he was standing before her blocking the light, khaki, chain-mail pullover, wide leather belt, black beret. Looking straight at his chest she said:

"You know who we are?"

"I can guess."

"Who we're holding?"

"The staff 'phoned details."

"We want Daniel Quinn, Peter McIntyre and John Fannin brought here before tomorrow noon ... also a helicopter."

He took out a notebook and began to write. She was tempted to say, can you not remember three names. She stayed silent. As he wrote the names he said: "Top-ranking chaps?"

"Trained killers like you."

Though his face was in shadow she could see his mouth stiffen.

"If not?"

"Can't you guess?"

"You'll have to say it."

"We execute one at noon, then one every six hours."

The officer repeated the names correctly, Lynam nodded and said: "Any shock approach and it's over."

Without warning he moved from light to darkness. As she turned to go up towards the front door the searchlight went off. Now, she thought, expecting a dozen soldiers to stampede past her through the door like a pack of rugby forwards. Nothing happened. She reached the door, went in, closed, locked and rebolted it and heard Leonard's voice.

"Well?"

"He wrote down the names."

"Rommel himself, what else?"

"Nothing, he listened and vanished."

"What did it feel like?"

"Being on stage."

"You did well."

Lynam felt braced, exhilarated by action and wondered how it was that she was less afraid to face guns than fire them.

"What now?"

"Watch and wait."

"Before I went out I meant what I said."

"Won't come to that."

They went into the living-room.

Alex Boyd-Crawford had moved from the table. Standing separately he seemed shocked, lost. Harriet went to him: He watched her mouth lipreading.

"Dear Alex ... come on, sit down."

"I'm all right."

"Are you frightened?"

"Perhaps they thought I looked dangerous ... do you think I look dangerous?"

"You look very much the bookish, kindly, broken-down landlord."

Alex looked into those eyes he knew so well. "You were pointedly rude at dinner."

"What did I say?"

"You know well what you said."

She shrugged and muttered, "All true."

He attempted a smile. "Real truth, my dear, leads to crucifixions."

Harriet did not hear. She was looking from Gallagher to Leonard:

"What do they intend?"

"Red chap wants to shoot us all, that's very clear."

Without looking at him she said:

"If anything happens you, Alex—me—any—or all of us, I want you to know how very, very dear you are to me."

"And the word you avoid?"

"You are very, very dear to me."

Gallagher now moved towards Alex Boyd-Crawford and flicked his pistol at him indicating the pantry door. Alex got up and shuffled out. Pacelli followed, taking the canvas bag into the pantry. As the door closed Harriet said to Millicent:

"I know it's happening, but I can't quite believe it."

It was Caldwell who replied.

"People near death experience similar feelings."

Harriet knew that he had said something apt, but the sound of his voice was so repugnant that she rejected the meaning. She watched for a response in her husband's face. There was none. Caldwell went on talking.

"As a child I remember being told how Christ had been crucified ... an Irish servant girl ... she told it well. I was stunned and said 'They were bad men ... they should all be killed for doing that....'"

She glanced at Caldwell and saw him nod towards Leonard and Lynam:

"That's how they feel, about you people ... they've never grown up ... dangerous deadly children."

Without quite knowing what she meant Harriet said:

"Out of the mouths of babes."

In the pantry Alex stood watching, frightened. Gallagher motioned him to sit. Pacelli groped deep in the bag, took out a small chemist's bottle and shook ten tablets onto the table. Gallagher brought a glass of water and indicated that Alex was to take the tablets. When he hesitated, Gallagher swung the pistol across his chest above his shoulder to inflict Alex, knowing that he would put both hands up protectively, an old monkey, defenceless before elemental violence. Gallagher dropped his arm as Alex picked up the tablets and swallowed them with water.

"Open your mouth."

Alex could not hear. Gallagher opened his own mouth to demonstrate. Alex complied. Gallagher peered in, nodded, and said loudly in Alex's ear: "Keep it shut inside ... your mouth ... understand?"

Alex nodded.

They went back to the living-room. Gallagher pointed at one of the two deep, wing-backed chairs at the fireside. Alex sat in one chair, grey, blinking at his smashed hearing-aid on the tiled hearth. The faces round the table watched, deeply concerned, questioning. After the initial exchange of looks Alex kept his head averted. Harriet moved from the table to the chair opposite. When he looked up she was asking with her eyes if he was all right. He made a small gesture with his hands, which said: "It's nothing, I'm all right." She nodded, relieved.

Gallagher winked at Leonard as he moved to the deep recess of the doorway that led to the hall. He sat in shadow watching the front door. The light from the bay window showed up the unreal pallor of his profile. Statuesque he hugged his knees, rigid, like a dog who has scented quarry and waits for it to break.

Leonard had picked up a chair and was now sitting alongside Lynam. An hour passed in total silence. The fire went low. Pascal added a few logs to the fire basket and examined the Tomkin clock on the mantel and went back to sit beside Pacelli on the magnificent couch in buttoned grey velvet. Side by side they maintained the same fixed half-smile as though permanently in front of a camera.

Alex had fallen asleep in fifteen minutes and, fifteen minutes later, Harriet. Millicent leafed unreading through a copy of *Homes and Gardens*. The Colonel and Caldwell were well through a bottle of Bushmills. Now and then they spoke in low voices. A helicopter passed low over the house, landed somewhere on the left. When the twirling blades stopped Lynam looked at Leonard who muttered:

"Couldn't be."

Another hour passed before Lynam said:

"This is deadly."

"What?"

"Everything. I feel sick."

"Nausea?"

"Not that sort."

"Want to read?"

"Couldn't."

"Drink?"

"Yes."

"Not wise."

"What is?"

"You should eat first."

"I know."

"Can you try?"

She shook her head. Leonard went to the table and picked up a tumbler. The Colonel poured a three-finger measure. Leonard nodded thanks, topped up with water and came back with the glass to Lynam. Without looking from the doorway Gallagher said:

"Slainte."

"Slainte leat," Lynam said.

"Want some?" Leonard asked Gallagher.

Gallagher shook his head.

"That's all you're getting," Leonard said to Lynam. "You must try to eat."

She nodded. He indicated Gallagher: "He needs it more than you and he's doing without."

"I don't need bloody lectures."

Five minutes later she said: "Sorry ... I feel odd."

"Not my idea of a night out either."

"The last."

"It's going to work, I can feel it."

"How?"

"Instinct."

From the chair Alex Boyd-Crawford muttered indistinctly:

"October ... no growth ... must finish picking apples before the frost comes ... they still bear ... old and cankered but still bear. My leaky cider press ... no matter ... nothing matters ... who's right? the Secretary ... the tribal chain gangs ... fraudulent ... or maybe me ... don't know ... know nothing."

When he began to snore Harriet went to him and did something to make him stop.

For half an hour Lynam sipped the whiskey. The ticking of the Tomkin clock became more insistent. The room seemed to lengthen slowly. Then she became aware of gradual grotesque distortion as the living flesh of each face turned grey in a fixed grimace of death. For a minute she thought she would scream as her caged heart leaped in beating terror. Normality returned.

"Can't we do something?" she asked.

Leonard thought for a moment, then winked over at Pascal and made a blowing mime with his mouth into both hands. When Pascal looked doubtful Leonard winked encouragement. Pascal took a tin whistle out of the canvas bag. When he began to play the expression on the faces of both brothers changed to one of rapt involvement, as the single note clarity carried not only its own beauty but a racial memory, evocative as the fields, battles and defeats—the music celebrated or lamented. Watching the lack of effect the music had on those round the table and aware of its impact on herself Lynam understood again why the first Elizabeth had hung Irish pipers as felons. The colour of melody neutralised the creeping terror of this ending day and the day that had to come.

The seeming naïvety of Hugh and Rosie McAleer's two sons masked, she thought, deeper roots, a culture old as pastoral Europe, clamped by history to the dead autocracy of Rome and the arrogant mess of the British Raj, themselves swamped now by the tinfoil gleam of Americana and the creeping threat of Russian paralysis, all beliefs and systems blending as old cultures died, inevitable and melancholy as the music, as the drying of tributaries with the deepening of great rivers.

At the table the talk continued in low voices, Canon Plumm turning up cards, Millicent now asleep on her arms.

"Haunting," Caldwell said.

"Noise," the Colonel said.

"Very special."

"Repetitive I thought."

"Do you know the language?" the Canon asked.

"No but ..."

"You'd like to?"

"It's the key."

"To what?" Canon Plumm muttered. "Bingo? Chicken in the rough, non-stop reels of jig-jig trash? The great, great show with endless whining lamentations manufactured by jackeens for plough-boys and shopgirls . . . what they want . . . what they get . . . what they deserve . . . Irish culture! My idea of hell."

Caldwell smiled: "God is not a proven Protestant, Canon!"

"Damnation for me," the Canon said, "if he's Roman Catholic."

"You grow a little acid, John," the Colonel said.

"Accurate and angry," the Canon said. "Hatred, they're good at that, and killing . . . they breed good killers, poor leaders."

Almost inaudibly Caldwell muttered, "Next to love the sweetest thing is hate."

The transistorised voice of a BBC news-reader came from the doorway. They paused, listening alert. It was too faint to hear.

"All so unfair," the Colonel said. "We were never absentees, my grandfather cut rents to half and nil during the famine, mortgaged the estate to feed tenants, Catholic and Protestant, one of my cousins signed the Treaty for the Irish side, Harriet's father was related through marriage to Lloyd George . . . lunacy."

He paused looking into his whiskey. "I knew Erskine well . . . a good actor . . . in his heart of hearts he didn't believe in nationalism any more than I do."

"Did he say so?" Caldwell asked.

"I could sense it . . . it's a disease."

"Sadly," Caldwell said, "most nations suffer from it."

"The cancer is in this room and may kill us shortly."

After a minute Caldwell asked: "Could we, should we try something?"

"If you want to die *now* Stuart, yes, but I think they'll let you go."

"It didn't sound ..."

"'Course they will ... doesn't do to shoot Americans ... ancient order ... strong subscribers."

"No special preference for humble churchmen I expect?" Canon Plumm asked.

"I doubt it John."

Gallagher's voice came from the doorway, bleak as a Derry street in January: 'Pity you're not a bishop, Sir."

In a very low voice the Colonel asked: "Could he have heard?"

"Apparently," Caldwell said.

"Unnatural."

"Every way," the Canon added.

Caldwell was about to say something when the volume of Gallagher's transistor was turned to a newsreader's voice in mid-sentence.

"... at the Armstrong Estate in County Fermanagh the Army are standing by. The kidnappers are demanding the release of three leading Provisionals from the Maze camp at Belfast. They want them brought to Inver Hall by helicopter. If this demand is not met, they say they will kill the first hostage at noon tomorrow and thereafter one every six hours. Colonel Armstrong served under General Montgomery in the African campaign and was awarded the D.S.O. Also hostage is Alexander Boyd-Crawford, member of the old Stormont Parliament for over twenty years. An American professor and a Protestant clergyman are among the six being held."

Gallagher switched off as the news-reader switched to the next topic. All awake and listening in silence except Alex. Harriet was the first to speak. To Millicent she said:

"We don't exist dear."

"I noticed," Millicent said.

"I published two poems in a school magazine over forty years ago, but I expect that's hardly newsworthy ... but you dear are a Bachelor of Arts."

She paused looking from face to face: "Bachelor? ... Should it not be a Spinster of Arts ... sounds miserable ... dog's nice ... who likes bitch ... bulls are magnificent ... cows stupid ... boars fierce ... sows eat their young ... the language itself is perverse to the female ... men only ... we're under sentence and the BBC don't know we exist."

Harriet's voice was a great deal less slurred than earlier, but she looked haggard.... Suddenly she asked Leonard: "What have you done to Alex?"

Leonard did not reply.

"He's a light sleeper ... drugged him?"

Again no reply.

Harriet went to the table and held a tumbler towards the whiskey bottle. The Canon poured a measure. She held the glass under the nose of the bottle till he splashed in another finger. Millicent was again trying to sleep with her head on the table. Harriet went round and whispered to her. Millicent got up and went to the wing-backed chair. Before sitting Harriet stood looking at the McAleers with detached curiosity much as people at a zoo examine creatures they have never seen before. The McAleers looked at each other, smiled, looked back at Harriet who continued to stare, till Pascal asked:

"Can you see horns Ma'am?"

"Pardon?" Harriet asked.

Pacelli said: "My feet are cleft, but we kicked football with the best!"

"Monaghan Minors '71."

Harriet understood nothing of what they said and muttered vaguely, "Yes", shook her head, sat down and turned to Canon Plumm.

"Was I rude tonight at dinner John?"

The Canon mumbled: "No consequence."

"I'm sorry."

"Nothing ... nothing at all."

Both the Colonel and Caldwell were aware that another apology was due. It was not forthcoming. Silence again and through it Lynam saw Millicent looking steadily into her eyes. She returned the look without hostility until Millicent turned her head and closed her eyes.

"Can't you let her go?"

"Who?"

"The daughter."

"Not yet."

Leonard took the empty glass from her hand, put it on the floor and said: "Your hands are ice cold."

"I know."

Quarter of an hour passed. Without looking at him Lynam said: "I want to make love."

Leonard did not reply till she asked: "Can we?"

"You're joking."

"Don't you want?"

It seemed to Leonard that the pitch of her voice had increased. He said: "Talk low."

"What?"

"Impossible."

She nodded towards the pantry and said: "In there."

There was a minute's silence before Leonard replied.

"Madness."

"I can't hear you."

"Insane."

"Sane ... we're dead."

"Far from it ... very far."

"Are you afraid?"

Leonard leaned very close to her and said: "Your voice."

"What about it?"

"It's carrying."

"Who cares?"

With a movement of his eyes Leonard indicated Gallagher.

"You might tomorrow."

"There's no tomorrow."

Leonard shrugged. The whiskey and seven hours of extreme tension had begun to tell.

"Try to sleep," he said.

She lay back in the chair and closed her eyes without answering. He was right. An absurd provocative notion which she would have welched on had he agreed. Why? To tempt him, humiliate herself, goad Gallagher, shock the atavistic McAleers, confirm the listening table in the poor opinion already held, or the reflex of a sad song and the bitter knowledge of betrayal, the total certainty that this was the last night of her life. Pointless trying to disentangle. Then she was in the pantry with Leonard, the door locked and she could hear Gallagher outside whispering to the McAleers:

"The Hound of Ulster is screwing the bitch from the Pale ... grave dereliction of duty boys ... they should be shot both of them; I'll see to it when the job's over!" Then she saw Gallagher go up to Alex Boyd-Crawford and shoot him twice through the head. Terrified she unlocked the pantry door that led to the hall, ran down the wide flags, opened the front door and out. It was grey daylight. As she ran down the granite steps she heard glass shatter. A single shot pierced a burning pain in her womb. She fell. As she tried to get up she was kneeling facing the bay window looking into Gallagher's cold face. He was pointing his pistol directly at her. She screamed.

Leonard had such a tight grip on her wrist that it hurt. She was trembling. Everyone in the room was looking at her except Alex Boyd-Crawford who was deep asleep. Leonard said:

"It's all right."

She saw the clock on the mantel—1.55—and realised she had been asleep for almost an hour.

"Did I... ?"

The faces at the table looked away, answering her unasked question. Harriet stood and moved towards the pantry door. Leonard said:

"Go with her ... and when you come back, eat, or take a pill and sleep."

She could sense real irritation in his voice. She got up and followed the Colonel's wife into the pantry. As the door closed Leonard motioned Pascal to stand alongside the door. The Colonel's wife had gone into the cloakroom toilet off the pantry. As she waited Lynam could hear, or imagined she could hear, retching. On the panelled wall someone had pinned recipes from newspapers and magazines. She tried to read one of them. The words had no meaning. She heard the toilet flush. The cloakroom door opened. Footsteps and the scrape of a chair and Harriet's voice saying:

"Do sit, please."

Lynam hesitated, then complied. It was a request more than an order, and she felt weak. She sat at the other end of the table facing the older woman, avoiding her eyes.

"Look at me please."

Lynam looked.

"Will you ... they ... shoot us all dead?"

"Depends."

"They won't do what you ask."

"They might."

Harriet shook her head.

"Nobby's not important ... old family but not important ... you're off target dear.... I know a dozen houses more suitable for this operation."

There was a considerable silence before Harriet began again.

"Odd how floods, bombs, hurricanes, earthquakes happen elsewhere to others ... never to oneself.... I wasn't sick with fright in there, I don't care when I die provided it's quick ... you know Milly?"

"We shared French tutorials."

"She's pregnant."

"I know."

"Told you?"

"Yes."

"Will she be sacrificed to Republican gods?"

"No."

"That's something ... I suppose."

Harriet studied the pitted quarry tiles on the floor for thirty seconds. Her face had the stillness and depth of an El Greco portrait, hurt, haunted staring eyes which a faint sudden smile now altered to subtle knowingness as she looked up to speak.

"French?"

"Sorry?"

"You did French?"

"Yes."

"What else?"

"Irish."

"You know David Greene?"

"Yes."

"Wonderful beard."

"He's a good scholar."

"Do you like Dylan Thomas?"

"Not as much as Kavanagh."

"Really?"

Lynam tapped the table then nodded towards the dresser and said: "I prefer this to that."

Harriet did not understand.

"Which to what?"

"Scrubbed deal to a Welsh dresser."

She smiled for the first time and said: "Yes, Milly read English and French ... but no real empathy ... *Henry the Fifth* troubles me ... do you like it?"

"No."

"Nor do I ... inexcusable of Shakespeare, bad as the Old Testament ... reeks of blood and empire.... Nobby loves it ... you're like a cousin of mine, Dolly Travers, incredibly like ... dead poor Dolly, happy life ... never married. Thought she wasn't happy but a hundred times more so than.... I feel quite exhilarated at the idea of sudden extinction.... Mother was accomplished ... the piano ... played with Paderewski in a drawing room once ... I was a child of eight ... And Paderewski said after it was the most beautiful rendering of a Chopin Prelude he had ever heard. Poor mother was radiant. Everyone clapped. Father was

Welsh ... shrewd at business. His money kept this place going ... his money ... my money...."

Harriet paused and studied Lynam for a moment.

"We're sister Celts, you and I ... I can sing a little ... though not much to sing about these days.... Would you like to get me a glass of water ... please."

Lynam brought the glass of water.

"After Derry I wept, you know, and Nobby was overwhelmed ... true ... he's human ... all of us ... very human ... so terribly sad what we do to each other don't you think? He tried to 'phone Frank Carrington ... couldn't get through ... retired Colonels in Fermanagh don't count for much ... rather silly really holding us ... he's liked ... always Catholics on the staff ... and what you're doing won't be popular with Catholics or Protestants ... of that I'm sure ... but you're here and that's it ... war is a series of unfortunate blunders ... like marriage."

She inhaled deeply on a cigarette, exhaling through her mouth and nose. She then finished the glass of water.

"That red-headed youth, such astonishing energy ... such hatred, are you like that?"

"No."

"Do you love?"

Again Harriet asked Lynam: "Do you?"

"Do you?"

Harriet studied the floor as though she had forgotten Lynam's presence. When she began it was as though she was talking to herself.

"Once upon a time a warrior went to war. When he came back he woke half dreaming in a grey dawn distressed and crying for a comrade who had died."

She paused for ten seconds, looked up and said: "You can fight the living my dear, not the dead ... marriage is such a cruel trap for some that they long for...."

She searched about her memory and found:

> *"That high capital where Kingly death*
> *Keeps his pale Court in beauty and decay.*

Shelley, poor boy ... why did I tell you that?"

"We're both dead."

"Yes ... Nobby says I'm maudlin ... would you like some coffee? ... I would."

"Where?"

Harriet pointed.

"In that cupboard, instant, the kettle's there ... power point beside the sink, we keep it here ... there's a mile of corridor to the kitchen proper.... What happened to Maggie Reilly and the Johnstons?"

"Pardon?"

"The staff?"

"They were locked out."

"Ah! ... Were they frightened I wonder?"

"I hope not."

"You're a feeling girl ... I could sense that ... Milly's cold ... my own flesh and blood ... sad."

Lynam moved about making the coffee.

"Your mother alive?"

"Yes."

"Father?"

"Yes."

"Family?"

"Two brothers."

"Like you?"

"Apolitical."

There was a kind of silence until Harriet broke it by asking: "What killed you?"

"Rejection."

"Always the same story ... one thing puzzles me, I can understand those who want to kill themselves, not those who kill others ... you look all wrong for the part.... Nobby's professional ... he looks right don't you think? ... Hatred is so sad ... personal hatred I know only too well, but to hate an entire people, race, sect or class, is so blind, so stupid, so unending, so universal, it makes one despair.... When that red youth smashed Alex's hearing-aid I knew then it was serious."

The electric kettle began to boil. Lynam moved to switch it off.

"Will they kill Caldwell the American?"

"I doubt it."

"Politically embarrassing."

Lynam nodded.

"They're embarrassing anyway, most of them ... he's a world authority you know ... medieval military manoeuvres or something incredible ... prestigious fellowship, a year's sabbatical, New England University.... Divorced ... said his wife was beautiful, but lacked a mind.... I think he thinks I have no mind ... could be right, I behave oddly at times.... Nobby thinks he's a genius ... met at the British Embassy in New York last year, some military memorial thing. John Freeman introduced them ... I think he's illiterate—not Freeman, Caldwell."

Harriet stubbed her cigarette on an ashtray and asked: "Do you think he's queer?"

Lynam could not answer. Harriet went on: "You can't tell nowadays ... nothing's certain. Has God lost interest do you think?"

"I don't believe in God."

"Nor do I.... Are the two dark ones brothers?"

"Yes."

"Don't look quite the full shilling do they? You've put down eleven cups, that's nice."

"Yes."

"Good idea. You don't say much ... perhaps you dislike me?"

"No."

"I embarrass you?"

"No."

"What do you feel?"

Lynam looked into the liquid lostness of those brown unhappy eyes in that blurred finely-modelled face. In ten minutes she seemed to understand the oblique confusion and compassion of this strange woman's mind better than she had ever understood her own mother.

"I must know."

"Pity," Lynam said. "For all of us."

Harriet continued to stare and the subtlety Lynam was aware of earlier returned.

"But you're here to kill if need be."

Lynam shook her head.

"Were you forced to come?"

"I can't explain ... sorry."

"Your hands are trembling."

"Yes."

"Are you afraid?"

"Yes."

"I fear death too ... did you believe me when I said I didn't?"

"Not quite."

The door opened. Pascal stood smiling. Harriet stood and left the pantry.

There was silence in the long room as Lynam placed the tray of coffee on the table. Harriet took a cup and passed the others round. Lynam supplied Pascal, Pacelli, Leonard and Gallagher. As she sat beside Leonard he said:

"You were a while out there."

"Yes."

"Talking?"

"Listening."

"Can you eat?"

As she looked at the food without interest, Pascal came over, took a silver serving spoon and put some potato and cauliflower salad on a plate. He pointed at the cold pork, tongue, and underdone beef.

"No meat, Pascal ... thanks."

"Sure?"

"Certain."

As Pascal spooned mayonnaise she glanced round at Leonard. He was staring straight ahead avoiding her eyes. Deliberately? She moved to join the brothers, Pacelli shifting on the couch, tucking his legs under tailorwise. As she ate they smiled encouragement. The food was distasteful and their concern overwhelming. It made her feel unworthy, fraudulent. As the feeling increased she stopped eating. The plate began to tremble in her hand. Pascal took it from her and pulled up a chair to screen her from the table.

"Ate a lough more Bella. The grub'll steady you."

As she began to pick at the food Pascal said: "You were a while with the ould one."

She nodded.

"Seems odd. Touched?"

"Strange," Lynam said.

"You'd know that from her talk."

In a very low voice Lynam asked: "Did I scream over there?"

"A whimper ... nothing."

"You dropped off."

"Before that?" she asked.

The brothers looked at each other pretending not to understand. Pascal shook his head: "A dream I'd say."

"Aye, you were asleep," Pacelli explained.

She looked from one to the other gratefully and said:

"You lie beautifully ... both of you.... Are you boys afraid?"

"Scared stiff," Pascal said. "The stomach's in knots."

"Constant fright," Pacelli added. "Natural."

"You don't show it."

"We don't let on ... it's there."

"Keep smilin' ... stick together."

Pacelli nodded towards the hunting table.

"You're fit to talk to those folk."

"Martin too, if he wanted."

"And Jack's afeered of nothin' in this world ... go to hell for his friends."

"He is hell," she said.

As she looked over, Gallagher's left hand went up slowly. He tapped his left ear, then pointed upwards with his forefinger, eyes dilated, a tense listening image.

The chalk-white face turned towards Leonard in the bay window. Leonard went and hunkered close.

"Hear!?"

"Nothing."

A minute or more passed before Gallagher said: "Rats on the back roof, four or more ... hear!"

As Leonard shook his head a slate, scrape, or noise of slip came down distinctly through the house. Five seconds of utter silence followed. Leonard looked towards the McAleers and pointed at Alex Boyd-Crawford. The brothers moved as one carrying the inert body to the main hall. This took place so promptly that there was a pause before it registered that something serious had happened and was about to change everything. Leonard moved back to the bay window. Lynam sat up very straight knowing what might now occur. Muzzy from sleep Harriet stood.

"What are you...?"

Half stumbling, almost sleep-walking, she moved towards the door.

"What are you doing with Alex?"

Gallagher blocked the doorway and gave a small flicking movement with his left hand in much the same way as parents dismiss small children who have broken their concentration. Harriet kept coming.

"I am not afraid, and will not sit by while ..."

Gallagher's pistol whipped across her face so quickly that those in the room saw only the effect of the impact. Suddenly she was on her knees facing the fireplace, a welt from eye to cheek-bone, blood in her mouth. The Colonel was on his feet, veins swelling in his neck. Gallagher said, levelling at him:

"If you want."

As he spoke two pistol shots sounded in the hall. Looks of electrified horror on all faces. Gallagher motioned the Colonel to sit by pointing with his free hand.

Still on her knees, Harriet seemed to be looking for something on the floor, a denture at the leg of the hunting table. Crying, Millicent recovered these for her mother. The Colonel and Canon Plumm helped her to the couch. From the hall the sound of the bolts being withdrawn, the door opening. The search-light was switched on, then switched off as the door was closed and rebolted. The McAleers came back into the room unsmiling.

Sick, ashamed, Lynam turned her back and stood looking at the design of the tapestry curtains in the high bay window. It was swimming before her eyes. Then Leonard's voice saying to the Colonel:

"You've got one minute from now to tell them outside and get back, and they've got three to get clear ... one more sound after, anywhere in or near the house, and we execute the next."

The Colonel went out. It was already breaking light. Under the bay window he saw Alex's prone body, a canvas bag tied over the head. The Colonel spoke with the Commanding Officer and returned at once. When he came in Millicent was placing a cushion under her mother's head. She had replaced the dentures and was holding a napkin over the gash in her mother's face.

Lynam went out to the hall. Gallagher saw her face as she passed and said: "Necessary."

She did not answer. She stood in the middle of the hall, the bulk of the armoured cars distinct through the front door. Near dawn. She could not display weakness in the room and would need time for composure to return.

"Don't stand there," Gallagher said.

She moved to the cover of the door opposite. The thing was to exclude totally the reality of nightmare that seemed to grow with the breaking light. In the other doorway Leonard was whispering with Gallagher;

both checking their wrist-watches, one looking up the dark stairwell, the other watching the door, both tense.

Coolfada ... the smell of the sea, the astonishing greenness of grass that grew in lumps from the thatch, the peace of the sky and all the cats named after saints and townlands. People came to the house every evening because her grandmother had the cure for shingles. Once she was allowed to sit in the creppy and watch. The old woman placed twigs in the glowing turf, withdrew them glowing and went round a woman's stricken face half an inch from the skin saying prayers in Irish. One summer's day, a neighbour man came with a mongrel terrier. When he was inside the terrier chased and caught a white kitten and crushed it with a snap. She ran with it into her Grandmother, screaming, warm blood on her hands. Her Grandmother wrapped the kitten in brown paper, washed her hands and went out to the potato patch. As she buried it, she said:

"Some dogs kill cats, some men kill other men ... the sea, hunger, disorder, old age, aye and a broken heart, night brings day brings night ... death comes ... don't cry love, it's life."

The one image of Coolfada that she had wanted to forget had jerked back now with sickening vividness. The blood was on her hands now as it had been twenty years ago. If Coolfada conjured images of blood and death, there was no refuge in memory. Her eyes were closed. She did not see Leonard cross the hall. She heard him say:

"You'll have to come back ... deadly out here."

When she looked he thumbed at the wide stairwell leading up into the darkness of the house.

"Did he have to be so brutal?"

"She's all right ... sitting up."

Leonard waited. Lynam ran the back of her hand up both cheeks to ensure that they were dry and went back to the living room. Gallagher had moved the two chairs from the bay window and now swung back the heavy curtains. He unclasped the shutters. As he folded them back Pascal switched off the lights. A dim light filled the room. Millicent stood, her body shaking, as she said directly to Gallagher:

"Bastard, sickly cowardly murdering bastard."

Suddenly she turned to Lynam.

"Are these your friends. A one-eyed dummy, two imbeciles and a sadist... ! My Christ, you're sick... ! All of you ... sick!!"

The effect on Gallagher was almost physical. For ten seconds he could scarcely speak with fury. The first words coming in a whisper: "Stuffed bitch ... your mind's feeble as your tongue."

Suddenly he shouted: "Why are we sick. Come on, answer. Why?! Let's hear, any, all of you ... come on ... why?! Answer ... you know it ... you are it."

In the silence that followed Leonard said quietly to the Colonel: "Your wife was foolhardy Sir. Lucky she's alive."

"That's arguable," Harriet muttered.

"I would advise you," Leonard said, "to warn your

daughter that she has no licence to insult ... that, for the time being, is our privilege."

The Colonel did not look at Leonard as he asked: "Is this how you treat prisoners ... wage war?"

Before Leonard could respond Gallagher cut in, his face rigid with hatred: "You talk of war and prisoners? You!"

He flicked his pistol.

"When we look for common rights the way you got your empire, all your lackeys in the Press and Commons yap; hang them, hang them, hang them. Mother of Parliaments? A fat knacker's wife who's flayed half the bloody world ... and you think the world is with you? Such shits they say ... such lying bullying hypocrites ... with your mock Monarchy and zoo-keeping Dukes and public schools, all stiff upper prick and regiments of back-street rats and buggering Horatios, you have deported, degraded, starved and tortured us and still do ... and no apology and never will ... but smirk and snigger at stupid Paddy, dirty Paddy,

Ugly superstitious Paddy,
Paddy drop-out, Paddy drunk,
Paddy half-wit, Paddy Punk."

Gallagher moved round the table as the words came savaging from his mouth. He paused at the end of the sideboard beneath an oil painting of a First World War Brigadier. Suddenly he elbowed a magnificent oriental soup tureen. It went sliding, spinning, down the long sideboard, scattering ornamental plates and silver before it shattered to the floor. With a back whip of his pistol he tore the face of the Brigadier.

"You smash us for seven hundred years, you haven't quit yet and you wonder why we hate you ... hate is a nothing word for what we feel."

The Colonel looked from Gallagher's livid face to the torn portrait and the smashed ware. A spitting mini-Hitler ... pointless to argue with such hysterical hatred. As he thought this he heard himself say coldly:

"That was an Irishman leading other Irishmen."

"To free small nations! .. don't make me vomit."

Gallagher returned to the doorway. Pascal and Leonard took up screened positions at the edge of the window. Pacelli sat at the far end of the room near the pantry door. Lynam sat in the corner alongside the Sheraton table near Leonard.

A quarter of an hour passed in silence. Nothing but the ticking of the clock and the gothic screech of a peacock. Harriet stood. Sound of smaller birds, the first signs of light. She knew this from innumerable dawns. She walked to the bay window, saw Alex's prone body, then looked away to the lake beyond the half circle of military wagons. Grey, utterly still, mist hung, autumnal as though waiting and aware of the coming winter. There were a few faint stars very high, and faint tinctures of pink and red. She had seen a painting once in someone's house all grey and black and although she knew something awful had happened, and that something more awful was impending, she forced herself to say:

"Daybreak ... Sunday ... reminds me of a painting I saw in someone's house. We sleep when the world's most beautiful."

"I wouldn't stand there," Gallagher said.

"Will you smash me again if I do?"

"Dangerous," Leonard said.

"Dangerous?"

Harriet looked with incredulity at the pistols and smiled: "Quite a sense of humour ... I like that."

She turned from the window and looked towards the corner. Lynam was glad of the grey, half light. Harriet quoted: *"L'aurore grelottante en robe rose et verte*. How are you?"

"How are you?" Lynam asked, scarcely audible.

Harriet's voice wobbled as she said: "Alive ... but lacking a dear friend."

She went back to the table and sat close to the wing-backed chair occupied by Millicent who said: "I wouldn't talk to them."

Harriet stared at the dead ashes in the grate and spoke with unexpected edge: "Alex was dragged out and shot dead while two military gentlemen sat by."

"Mother, please."

"Doing nothing ... there are times when one must do something regardless of military hand-books and personal safety."

Caldwell said, very quietly: "You don't seem to ..."

"I understand precisely what's going on, and what's likely to occur."

In the silence that followed Millicent covered her

face and kept it covered while she cried. Harriet put a hand on her daughter's head and looked over at Lynam. When the effect of the crying and Harriet's eyes became unbearable Lynam stood and whispered to Leonard:

"For Christ's sake Martin."

Without looking at Lynam, or back at the table, Leonard said: "She can go ... and the American."

From the doorway Gallagher frowned and shook his head. Leonard shrugged much as to say "they're going anyway". There was a silence before they adjusted to what had been said.

"Now?" the Colonel asked.

"Yes."

Millicent stood. When she had kissed her father Harriet held her face for a moment, looking as though trying to read or recall something. Very gently, visibly moved, she kissed her daughter's forehead as a mother kisses the head of a very small child. In silence Caldwell shook hands in turn with the Colonel and Canon Plumm. Harriet had walked to the corner, her back to the table. Caldwell approached to make his farewell. She took his hand without turning to look at his face.

Gallagher stood to let them into the hall, followed them to the front door, opened it, relocking and re-bolting when they were gone.

From where he stood Leonard could see them go down the granite staircase, across the half-circle of gravel and out of sight behind the armoured wagons. Harriet came back to the table and lit a cigarette. The

Colonel moved to the fireplace and stood looking at the Tomkin clock as though it contained some secret. The hands read 5.55. Canon Plumm, despite his fleshy face and bulky frame, seemed greyer, older, more exhausted than either the Colonel or his wife, as though he now fully realised that his calling would count for nothing in this ruthless double siege.

Gallagher went towards the pantry. Pascal moved to take his place in the doorway. Above the wood across the dark water the mist fell away leaving one bright star adrift in a metallic sky. Morning star. Lynam approached Leonard. Looking out and up she was aware of a numbness that swamped the nightmare hours and the coming fear. She wanted to pray but had forgotten how to begin or who to pray to.... Lord have mercy, Christ have mercy.

"Remember Benediction?"

Leonard nodded and said:

"I used to sit and look at someone's back waiting for the priest to say 'Morning star'.... That I understood, nothing else."

"Pagan at heart."

Silence.

"It's quiet."

"Very."

"Did it affect you?"

"What?"

"The crying?"

"What do you think?"

"I think you must be very strong or very cold."

Leonard shrugged slightly and indicated Pascal in the doorway.

"They're strong ... they've got God on their side, the Mammy and Pearse's ghost."

"Gallagher ... he's terrifying."

Leonard did not answer and she said: "Psychopathic."

"I can't judge.... I'm here ... so are you."

"Why?"

Leonard shook his head as though the effort of answering such a complex question was impossible. A tired priest of violence, she thought, who had ceased to believe in the Creed. As he looked at her now she got a sense of something else; enigmatic, obscure, almost frightening.

"You are annoyed?"

"No."

"By what I said."

"No."

"Last night, you're still angry?"

Again he shook his head. She remembered how he had said Gallagher would not waste words when it came to killing. Gallagher's racial and political bitterness were genuine. He was a natural mechanism of terror and disorder. He did not, never would, want peace and harmony. When it ended, and if the Leonards had control, they would despatch him. She realised now that Leonard's silence was more sinister, more frightening than Gallagher's savage outbursts. His surface warmth and ease masked an inner detachment, clinical, ice-cold. For the first time she felt utterly alone.

She looked back from the window. The Canon had his elbows on the table, eyes closed, supporting his head with his hands. The Colonel's wife was again in the wing-backed chair, the Colonel sitting alongside her. He was holding one of her hands in both of his. Lynam turned away, aware that she was intruding on something very personal. Harriet could sense emotion in her husband's voice as he said now:

"Always separate."

She thought before replying.

"Very ... I understand."

"I did say at the time and since that if ever ..." He paused.

"You proved less than husband and lover?"

The Colonel nodded and said: "You were free."

"Free?"

"Yes."

"I died that morning as a woman ... you do understand that?"

Tears from the blood-hound eyes came down each side of his nose, disappearing in the grey, clipped moustache as he began to speak again unevenly.

"I was ... am ... abject ... can say only ... that despite ... my very deepest truest love for you ..." He shook his head. "No words."

"Beyond words ... I loved my illusion of you Nobby."

"If we must die, can we die friends."

"Well said."

"You don't mock?"

Harriet shook her head.

"Friendship is better than love ... much better."

Again, as she had kissed her daughter, she now kissed her husband on the forehead, as humans kiss their beloved dead.

The pantry door opened. Gallagher came padding quietly down the long room. He had washed his face, damped and combed his hair and seemed, Lynam thought, alert, unafraid, almost celebratory. As he approached he said:

"Reading my face ... what's written there Lynam? Thug? Criminal?"

The repulsion she had felt watching him come down the room must have been evident. Gallagher smiled and asked: "Can we kiss?"

"Cut it Jack."

"I am Ireland. She loves me, she should show it."

Cunning logic to shame and establish her in brutal collusion before watching eyes from the table and wing-backed chair. Leonard had warned, and kept his back to her now as the warning stood roosting in smiling blackmail. She caught Pascal and then Pacelli's eye. If she refused and it caused Gallagher to explode it would throw Leonard and the brothers on a tight-rope. Leonard glanced at her and his expression read, "It's nothing, do it and be done with it". As she hesitated, Gallagher said, for her ears only:

"You wanted to screw with him four hours back."

His voice normal he said again: "A kiss ... no more."

As he neared she felt her stomach revulse. When their lips touched he caught her chin, inserting his tongue, his eyes open, staring. When it was over she felt defiled as though she had been kissed by a grinning corpse. She wanted to scream and claw with her nails at the mocking face. With a tremendous effort she controlled the churning in her stomach and kept her expression impassive. Emotionless, Leonard asked:

"Coffee? Can you make some?"

Lynam went straight to the pantry aware of Harriet's watching eyes as she walked. She stood trembling at the teak sink and rinsed her mouth out. "Why am I trembling?" she thought. "Death might be three hours away, less." It was unlike her that self-control could be shattered by a sick Judas kiss, unreal that she should react soul and body with such revulsion. Intuitively she could sense an otherness in that kiss, something coming, hidden; what? Gallagher, none of them could tell what would happen before or at midday. Filling the kettle it seemed to her that the woman she had both liked and pitied last night now seemed enormously enviable. The victims had a dignity. She had joined with executioners, the army of the damned. As she thought this she knew the thought was treason. Waiting for the kettle to boil, Lynam took out the pistol and looked at it without the repulsion she had felt the evening before.

At the window Leonard asked: "Did you have to do that?"

"She's soft, snivelling at the first whiff of action."

"That didn't help."

"I'm inhuman, a mindless killer, she said it, meant it . . . what's she? . . . a hysterical, gutless, middle-class yacker . . . and what's Burke at, sending her?"

"Good question."

"She could wreck it."

Leonard shook his head.

"I won't let her," Gallagher said.

Leonard felt the impact of this jostle. He did not respond. Gallagher would never lead. He had the racial defect to a marked degree; too personal. It coloured his every word and act. Deliberateness was professional and although he had an ulcer from worry, slept badly and doubted much, Leonard knew that he was professional and said now:

"Leave her be, Jack, she'll learn."

A BBC station-wagon came up the avenue, bounced onto the lawn and drove behind the half circle of Army wagons. Well in view, two men got up on the roof of the station-wagon, mounted a tripod camera and faced it towards the house.

"The eyes of the world," Gallagher said.

Leonard nodded. Gallagher looked at his watch, it was 9.45.

"If the boys aren't here by twelve?"

"We go ahead."

"We?"

Again Leonard knew what Gallagher was implying. Apart from five kills in action, he had executed, with cold efficiency, a Belfastman found guilty of treason. Now he presumed Leonard would ask him to execute the old man lying drugged under the bay window, half suggesting that he would use his position as leader to deputise the ugly work.

"I'll do that," Leonard said.

"You will?"

Leonard nodded. Gallagher seemed surprised.

"Whatever you say Commandant."

It was whatever he said and Gallagher would have to see unmistakably that he meant and did what he said. Three words prompted by an oblique question. He was now committed to action which he knew he could and would do against the instinct which prompted avoidance.

Canon Plumm was alerted by the sound of the arriving station-wagon. He looked at the time and then went to the Colonel and said something. The Colonel nodded and pointed towards a row of book-shelves. The Canon read the titles for a while, then took down a book and leafed through it for five minutes. Lynam came in with coffee and passed it around. As they sipped coffee the Canon said:

"Sunday: I'd like to give a brief reading, do you mind?"

"Fine," Leonard said.

The Canon sat at the head of the table, the Colonel

one side, Harriet on the other. He put on spectacles, cleared his throat and read:

"A heavy yoke is upon the children of Adam, from the day of their coming out of their mother's womb, until the day of their burial into the mother of all. Fear not the sentence of death. Remember what things have been before and what follow after. This sentence is from the Lord on all flesh. The time of death matters not, nor the place, nor the manner. Therefore be ready, strive for high ideals. Be yourself. Do not feign affection, neither be cynical or without love for in the face of all disenchantment it is perennial as the grass. Nurture strength of spirit to shield you in sudden misfortune."

The Canon paused before going on.

"In war and peace victims are many. Do not distress yourself with imaginings. Many fears are born of fatigue and loneliness. You are a child of the universe, no less than the trees and the stars; you have a right to be here, and whether or not it is clear to you the universe is unfolding as it should. Therefore be at peace with God whatever you conceive him to be. In the noise of life keep peace with your soul. With all its sham, drudgery, its conflicts and broken dreams ... the world is still beautiful."

In the stillness that followed the reading Gallagher said distinctly: "Introibo ad altare Dei."

Leonard responded almost inaudibly: "Ad Deum, qui laetificat juventutem meam."

Harriet had not come across this excerpt. Moved, she

looked first at her husband, then at Canon Plumm and said:

"Very fitting ... thank you Canon."

The Canon closed the book of selected Sunday readings, considered for a moment, then stood and walked towards Leonard and Gallagher. Without looking at either he said:

"I want you ... all of you to understand that while I abhor your methods profoundly and dislike your politics, I hold no hatred in my heart." He paused. "I have often thought and said ... things ... unbecoming a man of God ... we are what we are because of history."

Gallagher scratched his chin with the nozzle of his pistol and said: "History can be altered."

Canon Plumm did not respond. He held out his hand towards Leonard. Leonard had to change his pistol from his right hand to his left hand in order to shake hands. Gallagher hesitated before following suit. As the Canon moved towards the McAleers and Lynam, Gallagher said quietly to Leonard:

"Plumm velvet, his ticket to heaven...."

Leonard did not reply. As the Canon sat after this the Colonel said: "I would like to identify myself with what Canon Plumm just read and said."

There was quite a silence before Leonard spoke.

"You understand, Sir, that we are at war."

All waited for Leonard to elaborate. He did not. It was Gallagher who added without looking round: "You know what war means: or should."

Outside, Caldwell stood beside the British officer who was in radio contact. Twice he said: "I understand."

When he put down the military 'phone he shook his head. Caldwell looked away to the lake, looked at his watch and said: "They'll let them be slaughtered?"

"They have masks ... four pistols and three point blank targets ... lunacy to go in."

The August sun was now high over lake and forest flooding the long room with glorious light. Leonard stood at the edge of the window and watched Alex's prone figure, and the camera on the roof of the station-wagon. There was a light wind blowing across the water. The Tomkin clock ticked with unrelenting steadiness towards twelve. His heart slowed as he prepared for deliberate action. The three faces at the table were fixed in expressions of frozen fear and resignation. Gallagher was looking at Leonard intently. As the clock began to strike the McAleers stood. Lynam sat in the corner her face blank. Total silence as the last gong of the Tomkin clock faded. Leonard stepped back so that his shooting arm would not be visible. Holding his shooting wrist with his left hand he fired two shots towards the canvas covered head, pausing between each shot. After the first shot the body had twitched. It was now still. Gallagher nodded faintly. Lynam noticed a slight tremor in Leonard's hand as he inserted two fresh bullets, her mind empty as though some mechanism had excluded the brutality of fact. The McAleers blessed themselves. The faces at the table registered total incomprehension. It was the Colonel who asked:

"What? ... Why did you fire?"

No one replied.

Lynam became aware of movement and looked up. Harriet was standing in the window. Lynam could not see her face, but could tell from her back that she was crying. When the effect of this soundless anguish became too much Lynam went to the lavatory. She stood staring blankly at the Delft bowl with its throne-like mahogany seating. She was there quite a while, teeth and fists clenched against the rigours of trembling when the door creaked open. Gallagher. She recognised his jeans and desert boots. She did not look up and felt nothing. When he said without inflection, "You all right Lynam?" she kicked the door shut with both feet. Gradually she began to feel normal, blood running in arteries and with it warmth returning.

As she returned to the room only the McAleers smiled. She sat separately watching the afternoon shadow edge across the wide bleached floorboards in the bay window. The silence and purity of light, and the tension of stillness became so oppressive that she stood. As she did, a megaphoned voice bombarded the house:

"A word requested with Colonel Armstrong at the front door."

She saw Leonard nod immediately at the Colonel. She went to the window. Standing behind Leonard she could see out and down. With a dull nausea she saw what had distressed Harriet; Boyd-Crawford curled in the grass, an abandoned foetus wrapped in tweed and hessian. The officer said about three sentences. As the Colonel came back, Leonard went to meet him.

Lynam watched them walk to the other end of the hall. Twice they paused, neither looking at the other. The Colonel then moved away and stood looking up through the banisters at an Italian landscape hanging on the panelled wall of the wide, slow-raked stairs, waiting. For what seemed like minutes Leonard stood rooted, staring at centuries of wear on the flagged floor. Was he going to consult? It was clear that what had been suggested or threatened was unexpected. He glanced up, caught her unmoving eyes and almost immediately looked away and approached the Colonel. From the way they spoke, turn about, and listened intently, she had no doubt that some form of compromise had been agreed. She could sense Gallagher alongside her, alert, listening. Without looking at him she said:

"Can you hear?"

"He knows what he's at."

"Do you?"

There was quite a pause before Gallagher asked:

"Do I what?"

"Know what he's at?"

"We don't matter."

An acid comment occurred. She let it go. No time

left now for anything but the pervasive and increasing fear. What was agreed?

She had heard, or imagined she had heard, the word "Disarming" and saw Leonard nod. She stood back now as they crossed the hall, the Colonel in front. She kept looking in Leonard's face. Again she got the impression that he deliberately avoided her eyes. He said as he followed the Colonel into the room: "They're bringing them."

The McAleers laughed.

"Powerful."

"Good man Martin."

"He was right all along."

"He always is."

Gallagher smiled watchfully. Lynam's expression like Gallagher's was questioning. There was no triumph in Leonard's voice as he announced the release, and he seemed even bleaker as he said:

"I might take a drink now."

The Colonel poured. Leonard took the whiskey, walked away and stood by himself at the fireplace. As Gallagher moved towards him Leonard said with sudden sharpness:

"Keep watch all of you."

Gallagher kept looking at Leonard with a suspicion verging on menace. With reluctance he went back as ordered to the doorway. They took up their positions again. Lynam could not catch Leonard's eye. After five minutes she came over to him.

"They're bringing them?"

"Yes."

"When?"

"Soon. An hour, maybe less."

"Why did they wait till now? ... so stupid...."

Leonard shrugged.

"It's a trick," she said.

"If it is, we go ahead as planned."

Both Harriet and Canon Plumm were questioning the Colonel with their eyes. He would not be drawn other than saying:

"I think it's all right."

"Thank God," Canon Plumm said.

Leonard finished his whiskey and poured another. He had made up his mind, but the more he thought about it, the more doubtful he became as he visualised its execution. For three years his life had been one unnerving choice. He had grown accustomed to hard decisions, but this one involved very cold thinking. The killing of the first victim compromised his position. He left his second whiskey untouched on the mantel beside the clock: 12.30. The helicopter, unless they planned shock action in the meantime, should arrive at 2. He felt suddenly very tired. He went to the couch and lay down and closed his eyes. An hour passed. Then he heard Gallagher's voice at his ear.

"The snag, Martin."

He looked at Gallagher. There was no way of lying to that cold ungiving face, always a move ahead.

"We'll have to wait."

"The snag?"

"We must wait."

"You're lying."

"Tired."

"Not that kind."

"Careful Jack."

"They don't do things that way, I want to know."

Leonard looked at Lynam. He knew that, like Gallagher, she could sense something unforeseen, unexpected. There was no way he could tell them.

"I won't be pushed Jack."

When Gallagher accepted that Leonard would not be forced to speak he began to move. Leonard watched him obey then gave a silent whistle. Gallagher came back and bent towards Leonard who whispered. Gallagher straightened. For quite a while he stood thinking. Finally he nodded and glanced at Lynam with a look almost akin to compassion. As she saw this look a feeling of doom crept about her heart. What had been said? Was Gallagher a privy to it? If so why was she excluded:

"There was a deal," she said.

Leonard nodded.

"What?"

"Presently."

The Colonel looked up from a book called *Beautiful Flowering Shrubs*, by G. Clarke Nuttal, opened at chapter XVIII, "The Evergreen Rhododendrons".

He had read the same paragraph three times without comprehension. He now turned the pages looking at splendid colour illustrations. Now and then he showed a plate to his wife who nodded and said: "Exquisite" or "Beautiful". Canon Plumm continued with the *Selected Sunday Readings.* Now and then he pointed out a passage to Harriet who read, smoking continuously.

At ten past two they all heard the helicopter approaching. As it dropped to silence Leonard got up, nodding towards the Colonel. In the hall Leonard said:

"If they're here we take two of you as far as the helicopter."

"Disarming?"

"When you come back."

The Colonel went down behind the armoured wagons and was back in less than a minute. As he came in the door he said to Leonard:

"They're here."

Leonard went into the room and walked towards Lynam. He picked up her handbag, took out the pistol and put it in his back pocket. Baffled, half understanding, she watched as he approached Pascal and whispered. Pascal handed his pistol to Leonard. He then approached Pacelli, who also handed him his pistol. Leonard then handed one of the pistols to Gallagher.

"What are you doing?" Lynam asked.

Leonard did not reply. He walked to the Adam fireplace and stood under the great gilt mirror. Gallagher moved from the window towards the far end of the room and stood where everyone was well in focus. Leonard had obviously prepared and picked his words now with great care, speaking in such a low voice that all had to strain to catch what he said.

"The offer was nothing or ... three for three...." He paused. "The men being released you know about ... their value.... I had to choose.... I've chosen."

Lynam listened unbelieving as the spare words branded her accessory to murder, condemned her to the brutality and living death of a prison compound. Leonard was looking at Pascal and Pacelli as he said:

"I'm sorry boys.... Your mother will be cared."

He turned to Lynam. What he had intended saying now seemed inadequate. Suddenly behind those hooded eyes she saw meanness, cowardice and treachery. Before he could speak she said:

"Picked yourself! ... My God you're a coward."

She was on her feet, trembling so much she could scarcely speak. She nodded at Gallagher.

"Picked ... him ... before me?"

"He does what he does better than you."

He stopped himself from adding: "And so do they."

Her voice was shrill as she said: "Psychopathic and you know it."

"Then so am I ... I won't judge and I've decided ... I'm sorry."

"You're not.... The captain and the first mate leaving the crew to sink; they'll write ballads about you Commandant when you're court-martialled.... Coward and Leonard will rhyme well enough."

The words stung. What she said now had occurred to Leonard again and again in the two hour wait. He was certain that Burke and the military council would approve but regret his decision. Two bomb technicians and a suspect propagandist were nothing like the force, drive and dedication of the three men released. And he had to decide that Gallagher and himself were the most useful of the five. Enemies would whisper what she had just called him now, the only word that shames a soldier. The fact that he had killed before witnesses and cameras excluded the possibility of a chivalrous offer to stay. If one of the brothers had killed he would have chosen him to go. One way or another Lynam would have been left. Gallagher's voice came from the corner.

"This is not a cruise where captains drown with honour, it's war; he commands ... you obey ... that's it." Less harshly he said: "If you prize your life that much, you go, I'll stay. That goes for the boys too."

Leonard was about to intervene when Pascal and Pacelli said simultaneously:

"I'll go by Martin."

"Me too, Martin's right."

Gallagher asked:

"Well?"

"You mean it?"

"I mean it."

Were nice guys bastards, and bastards noble? Still unbelieving she looked from Leonard to Gallagher. Was he bluffing? She had only to say yes. As she looked she realised that Gallagher's offer was contemptuous. He was flaunting his prowess as a killer against her troubled conscience and humanity. Far from Carton country he was turning the screw with cruel psychological cunning, daring her to choose herself before him. To accept his offer would be vastly more ignominious than the grim, fast-looming alternative. She felt now that every word, step, and sequence had led inevitably to this moment of terror and rejection. Very quietly she said:

"I prefer gaol to either of you."

"That," Gallagher said, "is no surprise."

There was a noise of footsteps on gravel. Leonard went to the side of the bay window: Caldwell again on his way to the house. To the Colonel, Leonard said:

"We take you and the Canon."

Gallagher embraced both Pascal and Pacelli. From where he stood he directed his voice towards Lynam and said:

"Slán."

She did not answer.

When Leonard had shaken hands with the brothers he looked at Lynam. As he approached her she said:

"His offer was an insult.... I'd rather be dead than see you rule."

Leonard thought his thoughts. He did not express them. With his unaltering voice he said:

"I know."

As he turned to go, Gallagher took him aside. Sensing what he would say Leonard said: "She didn't mean that."

"She said it ... all she knows Martin ... who, why,

when, what ... they'll get it ... we can't leave her!"

"The offer is three for three."

As Gallagher pondered the reality Leonard said: "I've had two hours to think: this is the only way."

"I'll stay for one of the boys."

"You'll not."

"I want to Martin."

"Bomb technicians are two a penny ... you're needed."

"We're soldiers ... we should ... we can't leave them, Martin ... not both."

"When I move, move with me; ready?"

For ten seconds it seemed to Leonard that Gallagher would not obey. Without looking at him he asked again: "Ready?"

"Ready," Gallagher said.

Leonard motioned the Colonel and Canon Plumm to the hall. Gallagher made a pushing away movement with his free hand towards the brothers, a gesture of defeat and farewell. In response the McAleers stood and saluted. Leonard acknowledged the salute bleakly and followed. As they went Lynam sat lost, her back to the window. Gradually she became aware first of Harriet's eyes, then voice saying:

"A tale lamentable of things ill done
For the Living Dead: no comfort from the sun."

As Harriet left the room Pascal and Pacelli approached both smiling unnaturally. She stared into their faces.

"They'll brutalise .. torture us."

"Don't think on it, love," Pascal said.

"Bounce of the ball," Pacelli added.

"Some must suffer."

"We'll laugh five years from now."

"Aye to be sure."

"Show them you're not afeered Bella."

"Stand, you're a soldier."

"Put on bravery ... face them with us."

As she stood between them they kissed her as they had kissed her the evening before.

Harriet watched from the door as three camera crews filmed the four walking across the front of the Tudor house towards the waiting helicopter. When they were out of sight she went to Alex, knelt at his head and uncovered the face. The two bullets had entered his skull within the hairline leaving his face unmarked. She pulled off her shoe and propped it under his chin to close his mouth, shutting his eyes with her thumbs, aware of soldiers running across the gravel towards the steps. They ran past her into the house. Then a British officer was beside her on one knee holding her arm:

"Mrs Armstrong."

"Yes."

"We'll attend to that."

"I can manage ... a friend ... a dear, dear friend, so kind, a human being, do you understand?"

"Of course."

"A human being."

She shook her head. Alex's face blurred.

"I think you should come inside."

The officer was exerting gentle pressure on her arm.

"No ... I ... perfectly all right."

From her knees she saw the McAleers and Lynam come through the front door escorted by soldiers. As Lynam slowed to say something she was pushed roughly onwards by soldiers. Harriet bowed her head and wept. The helicopter rose from the side of the house, its blade whirling in the afternoon sun, a monstrous insect heading south across the quiet lake, meadow and forest.

When she looked up, the Colonel and the Canon were being interviewed by television reporters. Caldwell stood behind the camera crews watching. A reporter and a camera man with a hand-held camera approached the steps. The officer stood up and waved them away. They kept coming and he said:

"Please gentlemen, please ... later."

Harriet saw them coming, stood and said: "I don't mind, provided they don't show Alex like that."

They were three yards away now. The camera began to whirr.

"What do you want to know? Surely it's clear!"

The reporter said: "I understand you were brutally beaten Mrs Armstrong."

Harriet shook her head.

"Your face is bruised."

"Nothing."

"What is your feeling now?"

"My feeling? ... about what?"

The reporter hesitated, unsure. She waited till he asked: "A few minutes ago you were at death's door."

Harriet nodded. "Yes ... well ... my feeling."

She paused, apparently unable to go on. The officer shook his head motioning the reporter to cut the interview.

"No, no I can answer ... my feeling at the moment is one of ... desolation ... of unutterable despair ... that is my feeling now ... despair ... but look around you."

Harriet looked out over the massive shapes of war and the uniforms below, to the long lake, the great forest beyond and up into the August sun, the blinding sky.

"Look about you."

Her face fell apart as she said: "The world is still beautiful."

She nodded trying to smile and said again:

"Beautiful."